JACOB SHEA

AN UNADJUSTEDS STORY

MARISA NOELLE

CONTENT WARNINGS

This book contains themes and references that some readers may find distressing, including, but not limited to:

Violence — physical fights, injuries, and combat scenes.

Death — mention of loss and grief.

Abuse of power — manipulation, exploitation, and coercive control.

Oppression — class inequality and discrimination against the unadjusted.

Mental health — stress, guilt, and trauma related to failure and loss.

Parental loss and separation.

Body modification and addiction — references to nanite enhancements and their physical/psychological consequences.

To the fighters, the survivors, and the thinkers—your strength will shape tomorrow.

CHAPTER 1

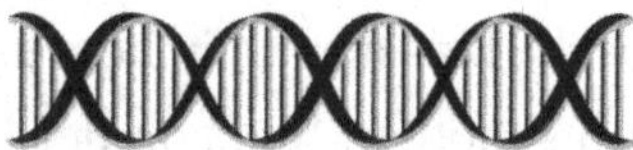

Jacob stares at the digi-board making promises of "your increased self" and "be the power of the future," wondering if that could ever apply to him.

His mother tsks. "What do you want with all that?"

Jacob shrugs. "Nothing." *Everything.* How much easier their life would be if one of them took a nanite.

With a suppressed sigh, Jacob follows his mother through the dojo's doors as the sun breaks over the rooftops. There are no students yet. Just him, his mother, and hours of work before the first class begins.

His mom unlocks the supply closet. Jacob watches her dump powdered soap into wooden buckets, the water turning milky white as she stirs it with a gloved hand. He grabs a mop without being asked. Two weeks into the summer break and he knows the routine. Not that he likes is. He'd rather be one of the students flipping people on the mats.

"Corner-to-corner today," his mom says, her voice still

thick from sleep. "Master Han has the regional qualifiers coming."

Jacob nods and moves toward the far end of the hall where shadows still cling to the corners. He slides the mop across the floorboards. Back and forth. Push and pull. His mind wanders as his body works. Thinking of all the kicks and jabs and chops the kids who train here use.

He glances at his mother. She's on her hands and knees, scrubbing the area beneath the weapons rack where sweat and dirt accumulate most. Her hair is pulled back in a tight ponytail. No makeup. She should get one of those nanites that smooths her skin out. But they can't afford even the lowest of levels. Not even an EverFresh.

The skin around her knuckles is cracked from chemical cleaners and constant immersion in water. Two jobs—dojo in the morning, diner in the afternoon—and still they live in a shelter.

"You have school today?" she asks without looking up.

"It's summer, Mom."

"Right." She nods, moving to the next section of floor. "You should get a summer job then. The convenience store on Pike has a sign up."

Jacob tightens his grip on the mop handle. "Master Han said he might let me help with the kids' class."

His mom pauses scrubbing for a fraction of a second. "We'll see."

We'll see. The answer that isn't an answer. Jacob returns to his mopping, gripping the handle so tight he almost snaps it in half.

Morning light soars through the windows, punching

holes in the shadows. The rows of practice dummies stand at attention along one wall, their fabric bodies bearing the scars of countless strikes. Punching bags hang from reinforced ceiling mounts. The wall-mounted weapons—staffs, practice swords, nunchaku—cast thin shadows like prison bars across the gleaming floor.

Jacob has memorized every centimeter of this space. Two years of watching from the sidelines, observing through the crack in the door while completing his chores. Learning from the whispers.

His mother thinks he doesn't see how Master Han looks at him sometimes. The calculating gaze, measuring his height, his reach, the way he moves even when just carrying cleaning supplies. Jacob pretends not to notice, but he is secretly pleased. Secretly waiting for the invitation to join the other kids on the mats.

A muscle in Jacob's arm twitches, wanting to move through the forms he's secretly memorized. *Not now.* His mother would see.

How many students take this place for granted? How many complain about the training, never realizing what a privilege it is to be here as something other than the help?

His mom rises from her knees with a barely audible groan. Jacob pretends not to hear it. Her pride is a fragile thing, and he's learned when to look away.

"The bathrooms next," she says, gathering her supplies. "Then we dust the trophy case."

The trophy case. Glass-fronted, spotlit, dominated by Master Han's achievements. Tournament cups, medals, certificates—all bearing his name in gleaming gold letters.

Pride of place goes to the World Championship trophy from fifteen years ago. Master Han making history as the first Korean American to take the title.

"I'm almost done here," Jacob says, pushing the mop into the final corner.

His mom nods, disappearing into the changing rooms with her bucket and scrub brush. The door swings shut behind her.

Alone, Jacob allows himself a single glance at his reflection in the mirrored wall. Thirteen, tall for his age, with his father's build and his mother's dark eyes. The man who left before Jacob could remember him still exists in the angles of Jacob's jaw, the set of his shoulders.

He looks away. He doesn't want to think about this. What could have been.

By the time they finish, every surface gleams. Every weapon sits perfectly aligned. The air smells of pine cleaner and furniture polish. His eyes linger on the center of the room, the heart of the dojo where Master Han demonstrates forms to his advanced students. The space where champions are made.

His mother's voice echoes from the women's changing room as she hums a half-remembered Korean lullaby. He has maybe fifteen minutes before she returns. Fifteen minutes when the floor belongs to no one but him.

He takes three cautious steps backward. One more glance at the changing room door. Still closed. One more check of the entrance. Still empty.

His heart kicks against his ribs. This is stupid. Dangerous. If Master Han caught him—

But Master Han won't be here for another hour.

He peels off his socks and tucks them into his pocket. He moves to the center of the training space, standing where Master Han always begins demonstrations.

Jacob steadies his breathing. In through the nose, out through the mouth. Just like he's observed the senior students do. He brings his hands together, centers himself, then slides his right foot back into the first stance.

Basic form first. Nothing flashy. He sinks into a horse stance, thighs parallel to the ground, back straight. His arms extend in a double block. He holds it, feeling the burn start in his quadriceps, the strain across his shoulders.

Ten seconds. Twenty. Thirty. The stance settles into his muscles, becoming easier with each breath.

He transitions to the next position, a front stance with a middle punch. He snaps his fist forward. The air parts around his knuckles with a soft whisper.

It's not his first time practicing. It's just his first time here, in the sacred center of the dojo, rather than in the cramped confines of the shelter bathroom, the only place with a mirror and enough privacy.

Jacob moves through the beginner's Kata. Each movement flows into the next, a river finding its course. He's watched the white belts perform this routine hundreds of times while dusting or carrying supplies. Has mentally mapped every step, every turn, every strike.

His reflection catches his eye. Not perfect. His elbow drifts too high on the knife-hand strike. His weight shifts too far forward in the back stance. But not bad. Not bad at all for someone who's never had a single lesson.

Sweat beads at his temples as he completes the sequence. The Kata ends with a formal bow, hands at his sides, eyes lowered. When he straightens, he knows he's not finished. He wants more.

Jacob shifts into the intermediate form he's memorized from watching the green belts. This one has faster transitions, higher kicks, sharper turns. His body responds with surprising willingness, as though it's been waiting for this moment.

The rhythm of the movements carries him forward. Block, strike, turn, kick. For these precious minutes, he isn't the cleaner's son. He isn't the kid who sleeps on a cot in the middle of a shelter. He's finding his purpose.

Three minutes pass. Five. He loses track of time as he progresses to elements of the advanced forms. This is where his memorization gets spotty. He's only glimpsed these sequences through doorways or while pretending to sweep nearby.

Jacob experiments with a spinning kick, turning his body and extending his leg in a sweeping arc. Not quite right. He tries again, adjusting the angle of his hips, the position of his supporting foot.

Better.

On the third attempt, he slices his leg through the air with enough force to create a soft whoosh. The kick would have connected perfectly with the shadow on the far wall if he'd been aiming for it.

He grins. This is what it's all about.

Jacob lands and immediately springs into the next movement—a high crescent kick that transitions into a low sweep.

It's from the black belt form, the most advanced sequence performed in the dojo. He's never seen it performed in its entirety, only in fragments during Master Han's private sessions with his top students.

He's mid-extension, his leg at its highest point, when a shadow shifts at the entrance.

Jacob freezes. Muscle memory screams to complete the motion, but shock holds him in place like a statue.

Master Han Seo stands in the doorway. He doesn't speak. Doesn't move. Just watches with eyes that miss nothing.

The silence stretches between them, tight as a bowstring.

Then, footsteps. His Mom's quick stride approaches from the changing rooms. Jacob finally breaks from his suspended kick, lowering his leg with an ungraceful thump as his mother returns to the main hall.

She catches him in motion. Her eyes narrow immediately, darting between her son and the master of the dojo.

"Back to work," she whispers, her voice carrying an urgency that makes Jacob wince. She crosses to him in four quick steps and puts a gentle hand on his arm, pushing downward as though physically returning him to his place.

The heat of embarrassment crawls up Jacob's neck.

Master Han steps fully into the dojo. Light catches on the silver threads in his black hair, on the embroidered dragon on his traditional jacket. His face remains impassive, but his eyes —his eyes are glued to Jacob.

His mom bows her head. Jacob follows her lead with a quick, reluctant dip of his own.

"Mrs. Shea," Master Han says, his voice carrying the faint

accent that twenty years in America hasn't erased. "The changing rooms are clean?"

"Yes, Master Han," she answers, eyes still lowered. "Just finished."

"Good." His gaze shifts to Jacob, lingers. Something flickers in the older man's expression—interest, perhaps. Or opportunity. "And your son helps you today."

It isn't a question, but she answers anyway. "Yes. School break."

Master Han nods once, sharply, then moves toward his office. Before entering, he pauses, looking back at Jacob over his shoulder.

"Your form," he says, "needs work."

The door closes behind him with a definitive click.

His Mom digs her fingers into Jacob's forearm. "What were you thinking?" she hisses, keeping her voice low. "You want us to lose this job? Do you want us to get out of the shelter?"

"He didn't seem angry," Jacob replies, his eyes still on Master Han's closed door.

"That's worse." She releases his arm and bends to retrieve her cleaning bucket. "He doesn't get angry. He calculates."

Jacob's pulse thrums at his throat. Not from fear or exertion now, but from a dangerous kind of hope. Master Han saw him. *Really* saw him.

CHAPTER 2

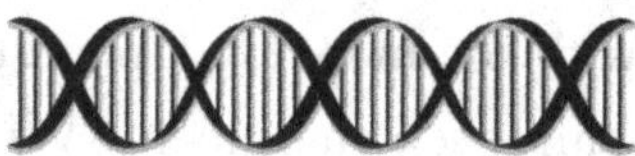

THE SUMMER DAYS drag on repetitively. But Jacob is happiest when he's at the dojo. He doesn't even care about the cleaning or dry hands.

He wrings the mop into the bucket, dirty water spiraling down in a gray tornado. His shoulders ache after days of continuous cleaning, but he doesn't complain. Complaining won't get him on the mat. Instead, he positions himself by the far wall, where he can see the advanced class begin their sparring. He cleans the same spot for a third time. Master Han stands at the center, his posture perfect, radiating authority without having to raise his voice.

"Junbi!" Master Han barks. The students snap to attention.

Jacob straightens his own spine, mirroring the students' posture. He tracks every movement as the class begins—the angle of their wrists during blocks, the pivot of their supporting foot during roundhouse kicks, the way they chamber their knees before striking.

"Jacob." His mother's whisper cuts through his concentration. "The bathroom needs attention."

He nods, reluctant to leave just as the sparring session begins. But he follows her anyway, dragging the mop and bucket behind him.

The men's bathroom reeks of urine and sweat. Jacob attacks the floor with the mop. He replays the forms he just witnessed, cataloging each movement. When he's sure his mother has moved on to the women's facilities, he props the mop against the wall and slides into a front stance.

He watches his reflection in the mirror, throws a jab, then another. His form is sloppy but improving. He's been studying for months now, piecing together techniques from fragments of observed classes. Jacob pivots into a turning kick, his foot barely missing the paper towel dispenser.

A toilet flushes. Jacob grabs the mop just as a senior student exits a stall. He returns to cleaning without making eye contact.

Jacob lingers as long as he can. The sounds of the dojo are heaven: bare feet squeaking against polished wood, the slap of skin against practice pads, grunts of exertion, Master Han's clipped instructions in both Korean and English, the rhythmic thwack of kicks against the heavy bag, his mother's broom bristles scraping the hallway floor, the distant traffic outside, his own heartbeat.

"Water!" Master Han calls.

Jacob abandons his dustpan and races to the cooler, filling cups without spilling a drop. The senior students barely acknowledge him as he distributes them, but he doesn't care. This close to the action, he can see the micro-adjustments they make between movements, the way they telegraph their intentions with subtle weight shifts.

One student empties the cup in a single gulp and drops it on the floor for Jacob to collect. Jacob bends to retrieve it, eyes never leaving the student's technique as he returns to sparring.

The days blend together. Jacob arrives at the dojo earlier each morning, leaving the shelter while the other residents are still asleep. He discovers that if he finishes the morning cleaning by seven, he can watch Master Han's private training session through the crack in the door while preparing towels for the day.

While his mother works in the diner, he is alone for evening cleaning. It stretches longer as he finds reasons to stay—reorganizing equipment that doesn't need reorganizing, polishing mirrors that are already spotless, refilling soap dispensers that are three-quarters full. His mother notices but says nothing.

A month after Master Han caught him practicing, Jacob scrubs bloodstains from the sparring mat. Someone took a hard hit during the afternoon session. He analyzes the pattern of the stain—oblong with a splatter pattern to the right. Probably an uppercut that caught someone's nose. He's becoming fluent in the language of combat residue.

"More force," he whispers to himself, reconstructing the blow that must have caused this particular mark. "Elbow higher."

When the dojo empties for the day, Jacob positions himself in front of the mirrored wall with his mop. No one to watch now. He spins the wooden handle like a staff, mimicking movements he observed during the weapons training session. The mop is unbalanced, the soggy head throwing off his technique, but he adjusts.

He flows through a series of strikes, adding footwork he's pieced together from different classes. He is definitely improving. His balance is better. His strikes more decisive.

"Again," he tells himself in the same tone Master Han uses with his students.

Jacob repeats the sequence, faster this time. The wet mop head slaps against the floor, leaving damp marks.

"You missed a spot."

Jacob freezes. Master Han stands in the doorway. Jacob immediately lowers the mop to the floor and begins cleaning the marks he just made.

"Sorry, Master Han."

The older man says nothing, just watches as Jacob mops. When Jacob finishes, he stands with his head bowed, waiting for a reprimand.

Instead, Master Han says, "The new shipment of practice pads needs unpacking. Back storage room."

"Yes, Master Han." Jacob bows awkwardly, unused to the formal gesture.

As the days continue, Jacob learns to anticipate needs before they're voiced—fresh towels appearing precisely when needed, water cups materializing as soon as students break from sparring, mats dragged into position before Master Han can ask. And he thought helping his mom in the dojo all summer was going to suck. But this is the best summer he's ever had. So what if he can't hang at the park with his friends? So what if Julie Conner went on a date with someone else? The dojo is the only place he wants to be, soaking up as much knowledge as he can.

He becomes a shadow in the dojo—always present, rarely acknowledged. But he watches. He absorbs. In stolen moments between tasks, he practices. A punch here. A block there. A kick when no one is looking.

Jacob notices the instructor's eyes following him occasionally. Once, when Jacob uses a subtle hip rotation to lift a heavy water jug, he catches Master Han's approving nod.

The smile stays on his face all day.

Another week passes. Jacob is starting to dread the return to school. He arrives at the dojo an hour before even his mother. He sets up the cleaning supplies, then hesitates, looking at the empty training floor bathed in morning light.

Just five minutes. Five minutes to try the spinning hook kick he saw performed yesterday.

He places his feet carefully, remembering the angle of the advanced student's stance. *Breath in. Focus.* His body coils like a spring.

Jacob launches into the kick, his body rotating through the air. For one perfect moment, he feels it—the balance, the power, the control. His foot whips around exactly as he intended.

He lands and immediately tries again. And again. Each attempt better than the last. But without proper training, how good can he actually get?

When his mother arrives, Jacob is mopping the floor. *Nothing to see here.*

His mom nods at him as she enters, surprise registering at his early arrival. "You're dedicated lately," she says, setting down her purse in the tiny alcove reserved for staff belongings.

Jacob shrugs. "Just doing my job."

He doesn't know why he's trying to hide it. Maybe because they can't afford lessons and Jacob doesn't want to make his mom feel bad about it. He'll learn on his own. It'll take longer, but he's determined. He chuckles to himself. Got that characteristic from his mom.

Master Han arrives next. "The mats need arranging for the tournament preparation," he says. "Show me how you would set them up."

Jacob is so surprised at the new task, for a moment he doesn't react.

Then his brain catches up with his increasing pulse and he rushes to the stacked mats, starts laying them out from memory, all while Master Han watches with his arms crossed and a brow raised.

Jacob finishes as the first students arrive. Master Han doesn't say a word and Jacob goes back to cleaning. But it takes him longer today because he keeps checking on Master Han, trying to read his mind, wondering what he's thinking.

By the end of the day, his hands are cramped from squeezing the mop handle so tight. But he's only too happy to stack the mats away again. He arranges them in perfect towers, color-coded the way Master Han insists—red for beginners, blue for intermediate, black for advanced. He's tidying the storage cupboard when the door slams open, and Kenji Park fills the frame, already dressed in his pristine black gi, black belt knotted perfectly at his waist.

Kenji scans the dim room before his eyes lock on Jacob. A

smile spreads across his face. Not friendly, but the kind that promises trouble.

"So, this is where the towel boy hides," Kenji says, leaning against the doorframe. He's Jacob's age but carries himself with the confidence of someone who's never worried about where the food on the table comes from. Or if it comes at all. "Master Han sent me for the new target pads."

Without speaking, Jacob points to a box in the corner. He returns to his sorting, hoping Kenji will grab what he needs and leave.

No such luck. Kenji saunters closer, inspecting Jacob's work. "You know, it's kind of sad. You're here every day, but you'll never actually train." He picks up a pad from Jacob's carefully arranged stack and tosses it aside. "This is a serious dojo, not a charity for shelter rats."

The words sting. Jacob grips the pad in his hands. He will not take the bait. He's heard worse at the shelter. From the other kids. From the staff who think they're being quiet when they discuss the "unfortunate cases" staying there.

"Nothing to say?" Kenji prods, moving closer. "Maybe you're just smart enough to know your place."

Jacob places another pad on the stack and reaches for the next one. His jaw aches from clenching it so hard.

Kenji steps directly in front of him, blocking his path to the shelves. "I asked you a question, towel boy."

"I have work to do," Jacob replies evenly.

"Work. Right." Kenji reaches past him to the pile of freshly folded towels on the counter. With a casual swipe of his arm, he sends them cascading to the floor. "Oops. More work for you."

The towels—fifteen of them, which Jacob spent twenty minutes folding—scatter across the floor. Some land in the small puddle by the sink.

Jacob's hands curl into fists at his sides. One punch. That's all it would take. One perfectly placed hit to that smug face. He's watched enough training sessions to know exactly where and how to strike. The fantasy plays in his mind —Kenji stumbling backward, shock replacing arrogance.

Instead, Jacob kneels and begins collecting the towels. One by one. Shoving the anger down deep.

"What, not even mad?" Kenji sounds almost disappointed. "Come on, towel boy. Show some spirit."

Jacob continues gathering the towels, refolding each one. He doesn't look up. Doesn't give Kenji the satisfaction of seeing the rage in his eyes.

"You don't belong here," Kenji continues, his voice hardening. "This isn't some community center where they hand out participation trophies. This is where champions train."

A towel near Kenji's foot is the last one remaining. Jacob hesitates, then reaches for it. Kenji's foot comes down on his hand, not hard enough to hurt, but enough to trap it against the floor.

"Know what I think?" Kenji leans down, his voice dropping to a whisper. "I think you're pathetic. Hanging around, cleaning up our sweat, pretending someday you'll be one of us."

Jacob looks up then, meeting Kenji's eyes directly for the first time. He says nothing, but something in his gaze makes Kenji blink first.

Kenji lifts his foot. "Whatever. Just stay out of my way."

He grabs a target pad from the box in the corner and leaves, slamming the door behind him.

Jacob finishes folding the towels, including the one that now has a dirty footprint on it.

"You don't talk to the students," his mom says on the way home.

Jacob is about to protest, when he catches the look in her eye. It's not anger, but something else. Fear.

That just makes him angrier. Who are these privileged kids who are popping nanites left right and center? Why are they so special?

He opens his mouth to tell his mom that. Closes it again. She works two jobs. They'll be able to leave the shelter soon. She doesn't need him mouthing off too.

The next day, Kenji corners him again. This time in the hallway outside the changing rooms. Same routine—insults, followed by knocking over the stack of clean towels Jacob is carrying. Same response—Jacob silently picking them up while Kenji watches.

"Don't you ever get angry?" Kenji says on the third day after upending a bucket of clean water Jacob has just prepared. "Or are you too scared?"

Jacob mops up the spill without responding. Inside, he's counting backwards from one hundred because ten doesn't give him enough time to calm down. They're both going to the same high school in September. There's no dojo there. Jacob is waiting until then to let him have it. He doesn't care that Kenji is a blackbelt. One good punch will take him down.

It becomes a daily ritual. Kenji finds him. Provokes him.

Jacob absorbs it without visible reaction. But each night, alone in the bathroom of the shelter, Jacob throws punches until his knuckles ache, imagining Kenji's face with every strike.

A week passes. Then another. Jacob's restraint never breaks, though it bends dangerously close some days. Kenji's interest in tormenting him seems to wax and wane, but never fully disappears.

One evening, Jacob stays later than usual. His mother has the night shift at the diner, and the shelter doesn't expect them until eleven. The dojo is empty except for Master Han in his office, going over tournament registrations.

Jacob finishes his last task. He glances toward the office door—closed, with light spilling from beneath it. Safe enough.

He moves to the center of the training area. Tonight, he's determined to master the crescent kick combination that the advanced class was practicing earlier.

Jacob begins with the basics. Strike. Block. Turn. Kick. His body flows from one position to the next with increasing confidence.

Then he attempts the crescent kick. His first try is awkward, his balance slightly off. He adjusts, tries again. Better. A third attempt brings him closer to the form he observed. On the fourth try, his leg arcs through the air with surprising grace, his body rotating exactly as he intended.

A soft sound catches his attention—the whisper of the door opening. Jacob freezes mid-stance.

Kenji stands in the doorway, gym bag slung over his

shoulder. His expression transitions rapidly from surprise to something harder to define as he takes in the scene.

Jacob lowers his leg, his face burning with embarrassment. He waits for the mockery, the cutting remark about the towel boy playing pretend.

But Kenji says nothing. Just watches, his eyes narrowing slightly.

Jacob returns to the cleaning equipment he left in the corner.

"Your form is wrong," Kenji finally says.

Jacob's head snaps up. Not the insult he expected.

"Your supporting foot needs to pivot more," Kenji continues. "Otherwise, you'll never get the height or power right."

He demonstrates with a quick movement, his own crescent kick perfect in execution. Then, without another word, he continues past Jacob toward the changing rooms, leaving Jacob staring after him. *Did that just happen?*

The next day, during afternoon training, Jacob brings fresh towels to the advanced class. As he sets them on the bench, he overhears a newer student snickering.

"Look at the janitor boy," the student whispers to his friend, loud enough for others to hear. "Bet he thinks if he folds enough towels, Master Han will let him train for free."

Jacob keeps his eyes down. He's heard it all before.

"At least he works harder than you," Kenji's voice cuts through the snickers.

The room goes quiet. Jacob's hands freeze momentarily on the towel he's laying down.

"What?" the other student asks.

Kenji shrugs, already turning away. "You heard me. Now stop wasting time, we have forms to practice."

As Kenji walks toward the center of the training area, his eyes briefly meet Jacob's. There's no smile, no friendly nod—just a moment of acknowledgment, a subtle shift in the atmosphere between them.

Jacob finishes setting out the towels and backs away, returning to his assigned tasks. But something has changed. A door has cracked open. It isn't friendship. It isn't even respect. But it's something. And for Jacob, something is better than nothing at all.

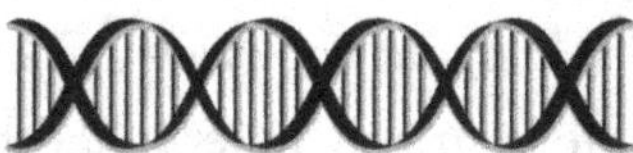

CHAPTER 3

Jacob smiles himself to sleep that night. But when he wakes and realizes it's only a couple of weeks before school starts, the smile disappears.

He and his mom walk to the dojo together. She looks like she hasn't slept again. She probably hasn't. The night shift at the diner runs until 2 AM, and Jacob knows she stays up checking the shelter's communal area for their belongings even after she returns.

"Before we go in," she says, her voice low despite the empty street, "we need to talk about how you address Master Han."

Jacob shifts his weight from one foot to the other, glancing toward the dojo. They're already running late after the shelter's shower line moved at a glacial pace this morning. "Mom, I know how to talk to people."

"This isn't just talking to people." Her fingers tighten around his arm. "Master Han isn't just people. He's giving us work when no one else would."

"Have I said something wrong?"

His mom sighs. "No. But you're thirteen. Hormones..." she closes her eyes and then snaps them open again. "You'll feel the urge to challenge authority. I'm asking you not to."

"I would never do anything to jeopardize your job."

His mom smiles and curls her hand around his nape, stroking his hair. "When did you grow up?"

Jacob smiles. He is already miles taller than her. And he's got muscles. And pubes too. Manhood is definitely on the horizon. He will learn to fight, and he will take care of his mother.

"Always bow to Master Han when you enter or leave his presence," his mom says, her voice taking on the formal tone she uses when discussing their Korean heritage. "Never speak unless spoken to. Address him as 'Master Han' or 'sir,' never just 'Han.' And for heaven's sake, don't contradict him, even if you think you're right."

Jacob rolls his eyes. "I know, Mom. I've been working there for months."

"Yes, but now he's noticing you." She takes his chin in her hand and gives it a squeeze. "That changes things."

A car passes, splashing through a puddle left by the morning's drizzle. Jacob waits for it to pass before responding.

"He's not noticing me. He just needs more help around the place."

His mom shakes her head. "I've worked for Korean men like Han Seo my entire life. First in my father's restaurant, then in every kitchen job since. I know when they're evaluating someone." She straightens the collar of his threadbare t-shirt. "He watches you when you're not looking."

Jacob's stomach tightens at this information. He's been careful with his secret practice sessions, or so he thought.

"Show me the formal bow," she demands.

"Mom, we're in the middle of the sidewalk."

"Show me." Her tone leaves no room for argument.

Jacob sighs and performs a quick, perfunctory bow, bending slightly at the waist.

"No." His mother's disapproval is immediate. "That's disrespectful. Like this."

She demonstrates despite being in her cleaning uniform and standing on a public street. Her back straightens, shoulders square but relaxed. She brings her feet together, arms at her sides. Then she bends at the waist, a smooth, deliberate motion to precisely forty-five degrees, her eyes lowered, head slightly inclined.

"Hold it for two seconds," she instructs as she straightens. "Not too long, which seems obsequious, but not too short, which seems rushed and insincere."

Jacob attempts to mimic her movement, eyeing the street to make sure no one is watching. What would Kenji think of this?

"Again," she says. "And remember what it means."

"It's just a bow, Mom."

"No." Her voice sharpens. "It's respect. It's acknowledgment of another person's knowledge and position. In Korea, this would be understood without explanation." She softens slightly. "Your grandfather would demonstrate for hours until I got it perfect."

Jacob tries again, focusing on the angle, the timing, the posture.

"Better," his mom says after his third attempt. "Now the greeting."

"*Annyeonghaseyo,*" Jacob recites, his pronunciation slightly off.

His mom corrects him, emphasizing the proper intonation. They practice until Jacob's pronunciation satisfies her. Then she teaches him "*Gamsahamnida*" for thank you and "*Jwesonghamnida*" for I'm sorry, making him repeat each until they flow naturally.

"We may not have much," she says when they finally resume walking toward the dojo, "but we have our dignity. We have our heritage. No one can take those from us unless we surrender them."

Jacob nods. His mother rarely speaks of Korea, of the family they left behind when his father brought her to America and then abandoned them. He wants to pummel her with questions, but she'll close up if he asks too many. So he listens and waits for her to drop new tidbits about his past.

They reach the dojo entrance. His mom pauses, her hand on the door. "One more thing. If Master Han speaks to you in Korean, even if you don't understand everything, never ask him to repeat in English. Just say '*Ne*' and bow. I'll translate later if needed."

"*Ne,*" Jacob repeats.

Inside, the morning routine begins. Jacob's mom heads to the office area to clean, while Jacob tackles the main training floor. But today feels different. Jacob finds himself hyper-aware of Master Han's presence as the older man unlocks his office and settles in to review yesterday's accounts.

When Master Han emerges from his office an hour later,

Jacob is replacing the water cooler jug. The heavy plastic container wobbles in his grip as he flips it onto the dispenser. Water glugs rhythmically as the reservoir fills.

"Shea," Master Han says, stopping a few feet away.

Jacob sets down the empty jug. He turns, remembering his mother's instructions. Feet together. Back straight. Precise forty-five-degree bow. "Good morning, Master Han."

He holds the position for two seconds—not one, not three—before straightening. He keeps his eyes respectfully lowered, not meeting the master's gaze directly.

From the corner of his eye, Jacob can see his mother pausing in her dusting of the trophy case.

"The demonstration class begins at noon," Master Han says. "We will need extra mats in the main room."

"Yes, Master Han. I'll prepare them immediately."

The older man nods once and continues toward the reception area. Jacob's mom resumes her dusting. When she passes Jacob on her way to the supply closet, she gives him a small, approving nod.

Throughout the morning, Jacob maintains the formal demeanor his mother instructed. He bows each time Master Han enters or leaves a room. He addresses the senior students with appropriate deference. The protocol feels less awkward with each repetition.

During lunch break, his mom joins Jacob in the small staff area behind the kitchen. She unwraps their shared sandwich, a tuna salad from yesterday's diner leftovers, and cuts it in half.

"You did well this morning," she says, handing him the larger portion.

"He probably didn't even notice."

"He noticed." She takes a small bite of her sandwich. "Master Han notices everything."

They eat in companionable silence for a few minutes. Then his mom says something in Korean, a phrase Jacob doesn't recognize.

"What does that mean?" he asks.

"It means *patience brings opportunity*." She wipes a crumb from the corner of her mouth. "My father used to say it when business was slow at the restaurant."

Jacob repeats the phrase, his pronunciation clumsy.

"Again," she instructs, exactly as she did earlier on the sidewalk.

They practice while finishing their lunch, Jacob repeating the phrase until his mom nods with satisfaction. Jacob gets up, about to head to the door, when he catches Master Han's shadow lingering nearby. It slithers away as Jacob rises. Interesting.

When Jacob emerges from the staff room, Master Han is waiting for him.

"Your mother teaches you Korean," Master Han says. It's not a question.

Jacob nods. "Yes, Master Han. Small phrases."

Master Han studies him for a long moment. "Good," he finally says. "Too many forget their roots in this country." He gestures to the mats. "Continue."

It's the longest personal conversation they've ever had. Jacob returns to his task, a strange warmth spreading through his chest.

That evening, as they walk back to the shelter, his mom

quizzes Jacob on the phrases she taught him. The Korean words feel more natural now, less foreign on his tongue. When he recites *"patience brings opportunity"* perfectly, his mother smiles—a rare, unguarded expression that transforms her tired face.

"Your grandfather would be proud," she says.

Jacob doesn't tell her that Master Han seemed proud too. Instead, he quietly practices another bow as they walk, perfecting the angle, committing the movement to muscle memory alongside the kicks and punches he studies in secret.

Respect and combat. Different languages for the same goal: survival with dignity.

CHAPTER 4

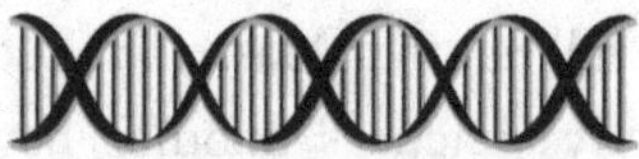

THE PUNCH COMES out of nowhere. One second Kenji is practicing forms with the other advanced students, the next he's sprawled across the mat, blood trickling from his lip. The senior student standing over him—Tae-Jun, national junior champion—flexes his hand and smirks.

"Sorry," he says, not sounding sorry at all. "Thought you were ready."

Jacob freezes midway through mopping the sidelines.

"Again," Kenji says, wiping blood with the back of his hand. His voice is controlled, but Jacob recognizes the rage simmering beneath the surface. He's studied Kenji long enough to read the telltale signs.

Tae-Jun laughs. "Maybe you should practice with the beginners first."

The other students back away, forming a loose circle. No one calls for Master Han, who's in his office with the door closed. No one steps in to defuse the situation. They're martial artists. They handle their own problems.

Kenji launches forward with blinding speed. His round-house kick nearly connects with Tae-Jun's head before the older boy blocks it with a forearm. They exchange a flurry of strikes, each connecting with enough force to make Jacob wince. This isn't practice anymore. This is personal.

Tae-Jun catches Kenji with a sweep, sending him crashing to the mat again. Before Kenji can recover, Tae-Jun drives a knee toward his ribs.

Jacob's moves before conscious thought appears. The mop clatters to the floor as he darts across the mat. He intercepts Tae-Jun's attack with a block he's only ever practiced in secret, never against an actual opponent. Pain explodes through his forearm, but he manages to deflect the knee away from Kenji.

Tae-Jun's surprise gives Jacob a split-second advantage. He pivots, grabbing the older boy's extended arm and uses his momentum against him. It's a technique he's watched Master Han demonstrate dozens of times. Jacob's execution is clumsy, but somehow, it works.

Tae-Jun stumbles forward, off-balance. Jacob continues the motion, turning his body to create torque. He hooks his foot behind Tae-Jun's ankle and guides the senior student in an arc that ends with Tae-Jun face-down on the mat, arm twisted behind his back in a crude but effective hold.

The room falls silent. Jacob's pulse thunders in his ears. Beneath him, Tae-Jun struggles briefly, then goes still when Jacob instinctively applies more pressure to the wrist lock.

"What is happening here?"

Master Han's voice cuts through the silence like a blade. Jacob immediately releases his hold and scrambles backward.

Tae-Jun rises slowly, his expression a dangerous mixture of humiliation and rage.

Master Han surveys the scene—Kenji still on the floor with a bloodied lip, Tae-Jun disheveled and flushed with anger, Jacob standing awkwardly between them.

"Explain," Master Han commands.

No one speaks. The code among students is clear: you don't tell on each other, no matter what.

Master Han's gaze settles on Jacob. "You. What happened?"

Jacob swallows. His throat feels like sandpaper. "They were practicing, Master Han."

Master Han's expression doesn't change, but his eyes narrow slightly. He knows Jacob is covering for them. He turns to Tae-Jun. "You allowed the janitor to put you in a hold?"

Tae-Jun's face darkens. "He caught me by surprise."

"*Surprise.*" Master Han repeats the word as if it tastes more bitter than coffee. He walks to the center of the mat and gestures for Jacob to approach. "Come."

Jacob remains frozen, caught between obedience and self-preservation. His gaze darts to the doorway where his mother has appeared. Her face pales as she takes in the scene.

"Come," Master Han repeats, his tone leaving no room for hesitation.

Jacob steps forward. He bows formally, just as his mother taught him, though his heart hammers so hard he fears everyone can hear it.

"You watch every day," Master Han. "Let's see what else you can do." He turns to Tae-Jun. "You. Spar with him."

The room stirs with whispers. Jacob's stomach drops. Tae-Jun is seventeen, with five years of formal training and two regional championships to his name.

Jacob glances at his mother. Her hands are clasped tightly at her waist, knuckles white with tension. But she gives him the slightest nod—permission, encouragement, resignation, all wrapped in one small movement.

Tae-Jun steps into position, a predatory smile spreading across his face. "With pleasure, Master Han."

They face each other in the center of the mat. Jacob mimics Tae-Jun's ready stance, adjusting his feet to shoulder width, raising his hands to guard his face. His palms are slick with sweat.

Master Han steps back. "Begin."

Tae-Jun attacks immediately. A jab-cross combination that Jacob partially blocks, though the cross slides past his guard and connects with his cheek. Pain blooms across his face, sharp and bracing. He stumbles back, regains his footing.

What the hell did I get myself into?

Jacob counters with a strike of his own, aiming for Tae-Jun's solar plexus. The older boy easily parries it and responds with a front kick that catches Jacob in the stomach, driving the air from his lungs.

He doubles over, gasping. The room spins. *Get up. Keep moving.* Jacob forces himself upright, circling away from Tae-Jun's next attack.

Time stretches and compresses. Jacob blocks some strikes, misses others. His ribs ache from a particularly brutal side kick. His lip splits when he fails to dodge a hooking punch. But he stays on his feet, applying everything he's learned from months of secret observation.

Occasionally, he lands a strike of his own. It's never powerful enough to truly hurt Tae-Jun, but it is enough to surprise him. Enough to earn frustrated grunts and increasingly vicious counters.

A sweep takes Jacob's legs out from under him. He hits the mat hard, air rushing from his lungs. Before he can recover, Tae-Jun is on him, securing a chokehold.

"Yield," Tae-Jun hisses in his ear.

Jacob struggles, his vision darkening at the edges as the chokehold tightens. He scrabbles uselessly against Tae-Jun's forearm. Panic rises, hot and suffocating.

Then he remembers a counter he saw during an advanced class—a hip escape combined with a pressure point strike. Jacob twists his body, drives two fingers into the nerve cluster on Tae-Jun's inner thigh.

Tae-Jun's grip loosens for a split second. Enough for Jacob to wrench free and scramble back to his feet. His lungs burn as he gulps air. Blood from his split lip drips onto the mat.

The reprieve lasts mere seconds. Tae-Jun attacks again, this time with a spinning back kick that connects solidly with Jacob's chest. Jacob flies backward, landing in a crumpled heap at the edge of the mat.

Pain explodes across his torso. Each breath feels like inhaling fire. Still, he pushes himself up on trembling arms.

"Stay down," someone whispers from the sidelines. Maybe Kenji.

Jacob ignores the advice. He makes it to his knees, then his feet, swaying slightly as he faces Tae-Jun again.

Master Han raises his hand. "Enough."

Tae-Jun steps back, breathing heavily but otherwise unmarked. Jacob remains standing through sheer willpower, his body a map of developing bruises.

"I can continue, Master," Jacob says, the words slightly distorted by his swelling lip.

Something flickers across Master Han's face. He approaches Jacob. "No skill yet. But spirit... interesting."

Jacob tastes blood and swallows it. His right eye is beginning to swell. His ribs protest with each breath. But he stands straight, refusing to show weakness.

"Where did you learn that arm lock?" Master Han asks.

"Watching you, Master Han," Jacob answers truthfully.

Master Han's eyebrows rise slightly. "Just watching?"

Jacob nods. "And practicing. When I could."

Master Han considers the information. Finally, he says, "Tomorrow, come early. Before your cleaning duties."

Jacob's heart stutters. "Yes, Master Han."

Master Han nods once, then addresses the class. "Return to practice. Tae-Jun, Kenji, office. Now."

The two boys follow Master Han, Tae-Jun with rigid shoulders, Kenji with a final glance back at Jacob. The look isn't friendly exactly, but it lacks the previous contempt.

Jacob bows formally despite his injuries, maintaining perfect form until Master Han disappears into his office. Only then does he allow his shoulders to slump.

His mother appears at his side, a clean towel in her hands. She dabs gently at his split lip.

"You'll have a black eye," she says quietly. "Maybe worse."

"Worth it," Jacob replies, wincing as she touches a sensitive spot.

His mom says nothing. She hands him the towel and steps back. "Finish cleaning the mats," she says, loud enough for anyone listening to hear. "Then ice that lip."

Jacob nods, accepting the return to normalcy. He retrieves his abandoned mop and continues where he left off, each movement sending fresh waves of pain through his battered body.

But something fundamental has changed. The students are looking at him differently now.

As Jacob works, he catches sight of his reflection in the wall of mirrors. His face is already beginning to swell, his lip twice its normal size. But his eyes—his eyes are bright with something new.

Tomorrow, he'll arrive early. Before cleaning duties. And whatever Master Han has planned, Jacob will be ready. Not as the towel boy. Not as the cleaner's son. But as someone who belongs on the mat, bruises and all.

CHAPTER 5

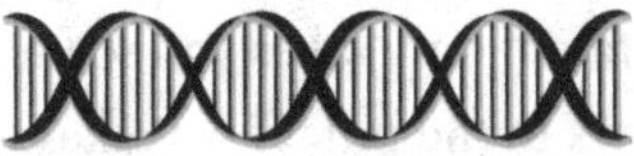

THE SMALL BLUE pill sits in Jacob's palm like a coin from another world, metallic sheen catching the fluorescent light of Master Han's office.

Six months of blood and bruises have led to this moment. Six months of dawn training sessions. Six months of perfecting forms until his muscles screamed. Six months of earning his place on the mat rather than cleaning it. And still not enough. Not in a world where athletes are popping nanites left right and center.

Swallow it, and everything changes. Don't, and stay exactly where he is. Living in a shelter. Talented. But not talented enough. Not with human limitation.

"Class Seven," Master Han says. "Reflex-Enhancement. Top quality. Not the knockoff kind they sell in Chinatown."

The nanite is smaller than Jacob's pinky nail.

There is no choice. No question. Jacob has already decided. He knows what he wants.

Master Han looms over him. The well-dressed man

beside him checks his gold watch for the third time in as many minutes. A sponsor. Jacob doesn't know his name, just that he arrives in a black driverless car and leaves with either a smile or a scowl depending on how Master Han's fighters perform.

"You have talent," Master Han continues. "Raw. Unpolished. But talent only takes you so far in today's competitions." He gestures to the pill. "This takes you the rest of the way."

Jacob glances at his mother, who stands by the door in her diner uniform, the coffee stain on her sleeve still fresh from her afternoon shift. Dark half-moons shadow her eyes. Her second job ends at midnight, but she still wakes at five to accompany him to training.

"The local championship has seventeen entrants in your weight class," Master Han says. "Fourteen are enhanced. The other three will lose in the first round." His finger taps against the clipboard in his hand. "The prize is fifteen thousand dollars. Plus side bets."

The sponsor shifts. "If we're doing this, let's do it. Tournament's in three days. Need time for the nanite to fully integrate."

Jacob has heard about nanites his whole life. The digiboards promoting miracle cures, enhancements, and transformations are all over the city. He can't deny he's always been curious, but he never allowed himself to dream that he could ever have one.

"How much?" Jacob asks.

"For you?" Master Han raises an eyebrow. "Nothing upfront. Fifty percent of winnings for the next year."

The sponsor snorts. "Seventy-five. Plus exclusive betting rights."

Jacob looks at his mother again. Her face is a battlefield of emotions—worry, hope, resignation. They've been living in the shelter for three years now. Three years of shared bathrooms and curfews and rules. Of folding their lives into plastic bins that slide under metal-frame beds.

"Are there any side effects?" his mother asks.

"Headaches sometimes. Minor sleep disturbance. Nothing serious." Master Han dismisses the concerns with a wave. And he doesn't mention the nanite deaths Jacob's heard about through whispers in the school hallways.

"Jacob," His mother says. When he turns, she gives him a small nod. Permission.

"Thank you for the opportunity," Jacon says to Master Han, then swallows the pill. Jacob has been training for six months. And six months ago that was all he wanted. Now he wants the tournaments, the trophies, the recognition.

Master Han clasps his shoulder. "Well done. Welcome to the winning side."

For a heartbeat, nothing happens. Then a warmth spreads from his center outward, subtle at first, then more insistent. His fingertips tingle. The fluorescent light above seems suddenly brighter, colors more vivid. He can count the dust particles suspended in the air between him and the gambler.

"Good." The sponsor nods approvingly, already pulling out his phone. "I'll adjust my position. He'll place now."

"Now we train for real," Master Han says. "Tomorrow, six AM."

His mother approaches, tugging at the collar of Jacob's second-hand tournament uniform—a slightly faded black gi with the dojo's emblem on the chest. Her hands smooth imaginary wrinkles.

"Does it hurt?" she whispers.

"No," Jacob answers, though that's not entirely true. There's a pressure building behind his eyes, not quite pain but the promise of it. "I'm okay."

She cups his cheek briefly.

"This is just the beginning," Master Han says, already pulling up a training schedule on a tablet. "Three days to prepare. Then we show everyone who you really are."

Jacob nods, the movement seeming to happen a millisecond before he intends it. The enhanced reflexes are already taking effect. The room appears in sharper focus. He can hear the sponsor's heartbeat from across the room, a steady thrum slightly faster than his mother's.

Jacob has made his choice. Swallowed his future. Ignored the fact that the sponsor is probably more of a black-market gambler. All that's left is to win. To make a name for himself. To be the greatest fighter in the world of martial arts.

The next three days blur into a relentless rhythm of drills and sparring. Every strike comes quicker than the last, every dodge a fraction earlier than he expects. His body is faster, sharper... more alive. And then it's time.

The Downtown Recreation Center smells like decades of spilled sweat. Fluorescent lights eliminate the shadows. There is nowhere to hide.

His opponent prowls the opposite edge of the mat. Seventeen, maybe eighteen. Twenty pounds heavier with muscle that comes from expensive protein shakes and private training. As well as a nanite or two. A smirk plays at the corner of his mouth when he sees Jacob, still slim despite six months of intense training, his tournament uniform slightly faded compared to everyone else's crisp colors.

Jacob breathes, centering himself. The air tastes different since the nanite. Sharper. More detailed. Like he can separate each molecule as it enters his lungs.

"Fighters ready," the referee calls.

Jacob steps toward the center. Time slows. Not actually, he knows that, but his perception has changed. The nanite working its magic, rewiring his nervous system to process information faster.

His opponent launches forward, a textbook jab-cross combination that would have connected three days ago. Now Jacob sees it coming. He slips the jab with a slight head movement and parries the cross with his forearm.

The crowd gasps. So does Jacob, internally. The movement felt automatic, natural, like his body responded before his brain could give the command.

His opponent blinks in surprise, then scowls. He feints a front kick and transitions to a roundhouse. Again, Jacob moves just in time, this time countering with a sharp strike to the solar plexus.

The impact travels up Jacob's arm, a satisfying thud of knuckles against flesh. His opponent staggers back, eyes wide.

This is so much fun.

Jacob presses his advantage, stringing together combinations he's drilled hundreds of times with Master Han. Jab, cross, hook. Low kick, middle kick. Each movement flows into the next.

The match ends in less than two minutes. Jacob stands over his opponent, chest barely rising with exertion while the other boy gasps on the mat.

"Winner, Jacob Shea of Seo Dojang," the announcer calls.

His second match follows a similar pattern. This opponent is more cautious, having witnessed Jacob's first fight. He circles warily, testing Jacob's defenses with probing strikes. But the nanite makes Jacob's reactions supernatural. He blocks, counters, and strikes.

When his spinning back kick lands flush against his opponent's ribs, Jacob feels a surge of something dangerous and intoxicating. Power. Control. And the anticipation of victory.

All those months scrubbing floors. Watching fights. Practicing techniques. How easy it all is now. The nanite has unlocked something inside of him. Highlighted his true talent. All those years of helping his mom clean the dojo... he couldn't be more grateful.

The second match lasts a little longer but the outcome is never in doubt. Jacob's hand is raised gain. The small crowd grows louder, people pointing, whispering his name.

Between matches, Master Han appears at his side, a water bottle in one hand, towel in the other. Finally, the treatment he deserves.

"Good," Han says, which from him is equivalent to ecstatic praise. "But you're signposting your left hook. Tighten it up."

Jacob nods, gulping water. The nanite has another effect.

He's not tired. Two intense matches, and his muscles feel fresh, ready for more. He suspects Han gave him a combo nanite. Not one for just increased reflexes, but at Class 7, they'll be adjusted stamina and processing speeds too.

"Last opponent is Kim Jun-seo," Master Han continues. "Fourth-degree black belt. Won regionals last year. He's taken more than one nanite."

"Weaknesses?" Jacob asks.

A slight smile curves Master Han's lips. "He's never faced someone like you."

Jacob's mother hovers nearby. She hands him a protein bar, which he devours in three bites.

The final match draws a larger crowd. Word spreads about the unknown fighter taking out kids with reputations for winning. Jacob hears snippets of conversation from the bleachers.

"—came out of nowhere—"

"—Han Seo's new protégé—"

"—definitely enhanced—"

Kim Jun-seo stands at the edge of the mat, watching Jacob with calculating eyes. No smirk. No posturing. Just cold assessment. Jacob recognizes the look—a predator sizing up unexpected competition.

When they meet at center mat, Jacob notices something he missed before. Kim's eyes track Jacob's movements with unnatural speed. Not just another enhanced fighter, but one running a higher class of nanite. A real threat.

The referee signals the start, and they begin their deadly dance.

Kim doesn't charge like the others. He circles, testing

Jacob with quick jabs and feints. Jacob snaps in a strike, Kim deflects; Kim drives forward, Jacob pivots, blocks. Neither giving ground. Neither gaining.

Two minutes pass. Three. Four. The crowd grows restless, their murmurs rolling like distant thunder, hungry for a clean hit. Jacob feels Master Han's gaze boring into his back.

Enough stalling. Jacob explodes into motion, feinting a front kick, then twisting, hips snapping, body spinning into a hook kick he's drilled in secret. The air sings around his foot as it arcs toward Kim's head.

But as he pivots on his supporting foot, something goes wrong. His ankle rolls outward with a sickening pop.

Pain explodes up his leg. Jacob lands awkwardly, nearly falling. The nanite dulls the worst of it almost instantly, converting agony to a persistent throb, but the damage is done. His ankle won't support his full weight.

Kim presses forward, forcing Jacob to move on his injured limb. Each step sends fresh spikes of pain shooting up Jacob's calf.

The match is slipping away. Kim scores with a series of strikes that Jacob can only partially block. The referee's attention sharpens. A few more clean hits and he'll call the match.

Desperation rages through Jacob's veins. He will not lose his first competition. He hasn't worked this hard for it all to end now.

Abandoning a defensive strategy, Jacob surges forward, closing the gap between him and his opponent. He grasps Kim's uniform. He pulls, twists, then throws his weight forward.

They both tumble to the mat. Jacob's ankle screams in

protest, but he grits his teeth and continues the motion, snaking his arm under Kim's chin as they roll. A choke hold, just as Master Han taught him.

Kim struggles, but Jacob has position advantage. Ten seconds. Fifteen. Then Kim's hand taps Jacob's arm twice. Submission.

The referee pulls them apart. "Winner by submission, Jacob Shea!"

The crowd erupts. Jacob rises unsteadily to his feet, balancing on his good leg. The referee raises his hand as the victory is announced over the PA system.

Through the haze of pain and triumph, Jacob sees Master Han across the room, collecting cash from the sponsor and two other men in expensive suits. Han's face shows no emotion, but his eyes gleam with satisfaction.

His mother pushes through the crowd, reaching him as his ankle finally gives out. She catches him, supporting his weight against her small frame.

"You did it," she whispers.

He did. But as the adrenaline fades and the pain in his ankle reasserts itself, one thought cuts through his euphoria.

He did it because of the nanite. And now he needs to keep doing it. With an injury.

A few minutes later, Jacob is sitting on a peeling vinyl bench in the locker room, a cold pack numbing his swollen ankle while something electric still races through his veins. He can't sit still. Nanite high, Master Han called it. Said it was the artificial rush that comes when your body does things it was never designed to do. Apparently the more nanites a person takes the less they notice it.

He's going to need more if he wants to beat people like Kim Jun-seo again. And win trophies.

"Can you wiggle your toes?" his mom asks.

Jacob demonstrates, wincing. "Not broken. Just a bad sprain."

She nods, adjusting the ice pack. The cold burns almost as much as the injury.

"I'm so proud of you," she whispers, looking up at him. A tired smile breaks across her face. "Not just for winning. But for not giving up. You did it."

"*We* did it." Jacob kisses her temple. "You taught me everything I know about discipline."

She squeezes his knee. They've always been a team, the two of them against the world. But today marks something new. Today, they won.

The victory replays in his mind. The crowd's collective gasp when he executed that perfect throw in his second match. The shocked respect in Kim's eyes during the final. And after, people pointing. Whispering his name. Not as the cleaner's kid or the shelter rat. But as the champion.

The door swings open. Master Han enters the locker room with a couple of suits. The sponsor and a couple of friends.

"—yes, three straight. No, the ankle thing was the last match. Kid fought through it." The sponsor's eyes flick to Jacob. "Gutsy. Worth watching."

Han is counting a thick wad of cash, peeling bills with his thumb. The sight of so much money makes Jacob's breath catch. More than his mother makes in a month of double shifts.

"Good work," Han says, not looking up from his counting. "The ankle?"

"Sprained," Jacob answers. "I'll be ready to train by—"

"Three days rest. Then light training only. No weight bearing." Han's voice is firm. "Can't afford to make it worse. Regional qualifiers are in six weeks."

Six weeks. Regionals. No more cleaning.

"This is your share." Han tosses a small white envelope onto the bench beside Jacob. "First of many."

Jacob picks it up. He peers inside at the stack of twenty-dollar bills. Three hundred, maybe four. More money than he's ever held at one time.

His mother's eyes widen at the sight.

"We'll need to work on your ground game," Han continues. "And that ankle will need support wrapping. I know someone who does sports medicine for the university teams. I'll set up an appointment."

The sponsor ends his call and approaches. "Kid's got potential. Raw, but the nanite suits him. Better integration than most first-timers."

Han nods. "We'll run a full analysis tomorrow. Optimize training to the enhancement profile."

They discuss Jacob as if he's not there. A commodity. An investment. But Jacob doesn't mind. He wants this.

"Can you stand?" his mother asks.

Jacob shifts his weight to his good leg.

"We should ice it again when we get home," she says, reaching for his gym bag.

Home. The shelter with its strict check-in times and thin

mattresses. But maybe not for much longer. Jacob clutches the envelope.

Han hands her a business card. "The appointment is tomorrow at ten. Don't be late."

She takes it with a respectful nod. "Thank you, Master Han. But I don't have the money—"

Master Han waves a hand. "It's taken care of."

Nanites. Medical bills. What else will they throw at him? But Jacob will take it all. If it means getting a place of his own with his Mom and winning titles, he'll take anything they're willing to give.

Jacob limps toward the door. The hallway outside is still crowded with people from the tournament. Heads turn as he emerges. A young boy tugs his father's sleeve and points.

"That's him," the boy says. "The one with the crazy moves."

Jacob's chest swells and he grins at the young boy.

A sensei from another dojo nods to him as they pass. "Nice work in there. That submission was superior."

"Thanks," Jacob says.

Outside, the evening air hits Jacob's face, cooling the sweat that still clings to his hairline. His mom helps him into a taxi—the first one he's ever been in—and gives the driver the address for the shelter. As the car pulls away, Jacob watches the recreation center recede through the back window and a secret smile spreads across his face.

Six weeks until regionals. Larger purses. Bigger crowds. More recognition.

He'll need another nanite. Something bigger. Something better. Something... more.

CHAPTER 6

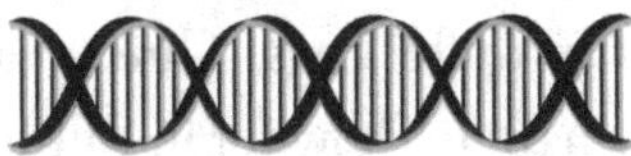

THE CARDBOARD BOX digs into Jacob's palms as he hauls it up the narrow staircase. Three flights up, no elevator. But it doesn't matter. He no longer has to live at the shelter. Finally, he and his mom have four walls to call their own.

"Almost there," his mom calls from below, her voice strained under the weight of her own box.

Jacob pushes through the door at the top landing, already propped open with a brick. The apartment stretches before him. There's more space than he's seen in years. Two bedrooms. One bathroom. A kitchen with appliances. A large open-plan living room. And it's theirs. Rent free, courtesy of Master Han.

He sets the box down and moves to the window. From here, he can see the dojo entrance below, the sign with Master Han's name in bold characters. Students filter in for the afternoon class. Jacob touches the new tattoo on his bicep. A swirling digi-tattoo, its shape and lettering changing to reveal messages of perseverance and determination. It's the first thing he's ever bought himself.

His mother appears behind him. "Three more boxes in the taxi," she says, wiping sweat from her forehead.

Jacob nods. "I'll get them."

Fifteen minutes later, their entire life sits in five cardboard boxes and two duffel bags. Three years in the shelter, and this is all they have to show for it. But Jacob doesn't care. What matters isn't what they brought, but where they are now.

His mother opens a box marked "KITCHEN" in careful block letters. She pulls out two plates, three cups, a handful of mismatched silverware. Each item finds its place in the empty cupboards.

"No more shelters," she says in Korean.

Jacob stands at the window again, watching a group of teenagers enter the dojo under an overcast sky. Saturday afternoon class—intermediate level. He recognizes their faces. He used to clean the mats they train on.

His ankle aches a little. Mostly when it's cold. Or sometimes in the middle of the night. There's nothing structurally wrong, the doctor had pointed out. But sometimes injuries leave an imprint on our bodies.

Whatever. It doesn't slow Jacob down. It's been six weeks since that tournament, he's won three more. The roll of bills in his sock drawer grows fatter each time. Not enough for luxury, but enough for this small apartment. Enough for his mother to quit her second job at the diner.

"We should get a couch," Jacob says, still facing the

window. "One of those L-shaped ones. It could go against that wall."

His mother doesn't answer. When he turns, he finds her holding a framed photograph—the only one they own. His father, his mother, and baby Jacob, standing before a restaurant that closed a decade ago. Before everything fell apart. She traces her finger over the glass.

"Maybe," she finally says. "Once we're settled."

A sharp rap on the open door startles them both. Master Han stands in the doorway.

"Master Han," his mom says, quickly setting down the photograph and bowing deeply. "Please, come in."

Han steps inside, his eyes sweeping the space in a quick assessment. His gaze lands on Jacob, narrowing slightly as he notices him rubbing his ankle.

"Is there still pain?" he asks.

Jacob attempts a smile. "Only when it rains."

Han nods once. He moves further into the apartment, hands clasped behind his back like he's inspecting a dojo, not someone's home. "This unit hasn't been occupied in three years. The last tenant was difficult. Complained about the noise from the dojo."

"We won't complain," she assures him quickly. "We're grateful for the opportunity."

Han's lips quirk in what might be a smile on anyone else. "Of course not. Your son creates half the noise." He turns to Jacob. "Tomorrow, 6 AM. We start a new program."

Jacob straighten. "Yes, Master Han."

Han gives a curt nod and turns to leave, then pauses at

the door. "The regional championship is in five weeks. Your weight class has two previous nanite champions registered."

His eyes flick to Jacob's ankle. "You'll have to ignore the rain."

The door closes behind him with a decisive click. Jacob releases a breath.

A flicker of worry crosses his mother's face, then she turns back to the box, resuming her unpacking, humming a traditional song from her childhood. One Jacob hasn't heard in years.

Jacob returns to the window. Below, Master Han emerges onto the sidewalk. A black car pulls up, and Han slides into the passenger seat. A sponsor, no doubt. Of the cash variety.

The rain starts, a light drizzle that darkens the pavement. Jacob's ankle aches in response. A phantom pain. It doesn't inhibit his performance.

His mother continues humming as she moves around the kitchen, finding homes for their few possessions. They've survived so long for so little. But now they have a door that locks, windows that belong to them, walls that separate them from strangers.

No more shelters.

The price is 6 AM trainings and pills that make his blood feel electric. The price is being owned, at least a little bit, by a man who sees him as an investment. But Jacob has a plan. He'll work so hard and win so many damn trophies, that Master Han won't be able to touch him.

After five months in the apartment and more of 6AM training sessions, Jacob wouldn't give it up for anything.

He moves through basic forms, his reflection multiplied in the wall of mirrors. The original reflex enhancement has fully integrated with his nervous system. Sometimes he forgets where Jacob ends and the nanite begins. He's acquired a few new digi-tattoos and then he found some lower class nanites that have given him reptilian eyes and a forked tongue. The combination works every time to put the fear in his opponents.

The door slides open. Master Han enters, a bamboo stick in one hand.

"Again," he says without greeting. "Your right elbow drifts."

Jacob resets his stance and begins the form sequence again. Ten movements into the thirty-six-movement pattern, the bamboo stick taps sharply against his elbow, forcing it two millimeters lower. The sting is brief but effective.

"Again."

This becomes the rhythm of Jacob's days. Again. Again. Again. Until perfection isn't a goal but the only acceptable outcome. He wouldn't have it any other way. If he wants the number one spot—and he does—then this is the dedication and perseverance it takes. As his tattoos say.

Weeks blur together. Winter melts into spring. Jacob turns sixteen with little fanfare. His mother makes seaweed soup for breakfast before her shift at an office building where she now works as a receptionist. Master Han acknowledges the occasion by adding fifteen minutes of meditation to the end of training.

Jacob's body changes with the seasons. Muscles define themselves across his chest and shoulders. His stance widens to accommodate new height. The nanite adapts with him, enhancing reflexes that are already becoming legendary in local competitive circuits.

One morning, Jacob arrives to find three senior students waiting alongside Master Han. All black belts. All previous champions. All older, bigger.

"Three-on-one," Master Han says. "Real contact. Begin."

They circle Jacob like wolves. He doesn't wait for them to attack. He assesses with his increased processing skills—a weight shift from the one on the left, a tensing jaw from the one on the right, a subtle tell in the center opponent's eyes. With a flick of his forked tongue, Jacob moves first.

His foot connects with the left opponent's ribs before the man can even raise his guard. A pivot, a strike to the second's throat—pulled at the last millisecond to avoid real damage, but enough to send him stumbling backward. The third manages a kick that Jacob catches, twisting the leg until its owner falls.

Twenty seconds. Three opponents neutralized. And they all had enhancements.

"Again," Master Han says. "They won't underestimate you this time."

By the fifth round, all four of them are drenched in sweat. Except Jacob doesn't feel tired. The nanite keeps his muscles fresh, his mind alert. He could go for hours.

The senior students leave with bruised bodies and raised eyebrows. Two men in expensive suits enter in their wake.

Jacob has seen them before at tournaments and exhibitions. They come to watch. To evaluate. To bet.

"Impressive," one says to Master Han, not bothering to lower his voice. "I've never seen a nanite so well integrated."

"Told you," the other responds. "Worth every credit. But the Zhang kid has the new Class Eight combat suite. Will the reflex package be enough?"

Master Han smiles thinly. "We're addressing that. Watch."

More training. More perfection. More men in suits appearing at the edges of Jacob's awareness. Sometimes they bring trainers from rival dojos, or fighters from professional circuits, and once even a military official who watched with particular interest.

Jacob learns to ignore them, to focus only on the opponent before him, the form to perfect, the technique to master. But he hears the whispers. The odds. The stakes. The money that changes hands based on what his body can do.

One morning, Jacob arrives to find Master Han alone in the center of the dojo. No other students. No suited men. Just Han and a small lacquered box sitting in his palm.

"Your progress is commendable," Han says. "But the regional championship approaches. Your opponents have upgraded."

Jacob stands at attention, sweat already cooling on his skin from his pre-dawn workout. "I'm ready, Master Han."

"No." Han's voice is flat. "You're not."

He places the box in Jacob's hands. Jacob opens it. Inside, nestled in black velvet, lies a small blue pill. This is what will give him the edge.

"Class Seven speed nanite," Han says. "Latest generation. Free of charge." His thin smile returns. "Consider it an investment."

Jacob stares at the pill. He knows what it will do—accelerate his neural pathways beyond the reflex enhancement, allow him to move at speeds that blur normal human perception. He's seen the videos of speed-enhanced fighters. They don't just win matches. They humiliate opponents who appear to be moving in slow motion. This is his ticket to the top.

"The regional tournament has a 60% nanite participation rate. And increasing every day," Han continues. "Reflex enhancement alone won't be enough anymore. Not at this level."

Jacob thinks of their apartment upstairs. His mother's smile when she returned from her new job. The college applications in his desk drawer—a future that once seemed impossible, now within reach if the winnings continue.

"Absolutely. Any side effects?"

"Temporary insomnia. Increased appetite." Han waves a dismissive hand. "Nothing you can't handle."

"Let's do it." Jacob lifts the pill. He places the nanite on his tongue. Swallows without water.

He inhales. Then, like a match struck in a dark room, something ignites in his bloodstream. The world around him slows. Colors sharpen to painful clarity. He can count the dust motes in the beam of sunlight through the window, track the nearly imperceptible movements of Master Han's chest as he breathes.

"Stand," Han commands.

Jacob rises. Or tries to. His intention and his body's response are disjointed, the movement too quick, sending him a foot higher than intended. He lands awkwardly, stumbling before finding balance.

Han nods, satisfaction gleaming in his eyes. "Adjustment period. Twenty-four hours. No training today. Tomorrow we begin calibration."

Jacob bows, the movement happening faster than he intends. His perceptions and his motor control are misaligned, like trying to draw while looking in a mirror

"Thank you, Master Han," he says, his words slurring together.

Han dismisses him with a wave. Jacob climbs the stairs to the apartment, his min on his future tournaments, on the shine of the trophies he'll win.

CHAPTER 7

THE REGIONAL CHAMPIONSHIP scoreboard flashes Jacob's name alongside fifteen others. By tonight, only one name will remain.

Jacob stands in the warm-up area, rolling his shoulders. It's been six weeks since the speed enhancement joined the reflex package and he's never felt better.

Master Han adjusts the collar of Jacob's competition uniform. "First opponent relies on strength. Second on technique. Neither matters." He steps back, assessing Jacob like a weapon he's just fine-tuned. "They can't match your speed."

Jacob nods. Words waste energy. Energy is for fighting.

The announcer calls his name. Jacob walks onto the competition floor, the lights spotlighting his arrival. His first opponent stands across the mat—eighteen, stocky, and radiating confidence. Jacob recalls the list of nanites of his opponents. This guy has a Class 5 strength augmentation. Outdated. Inadequate.

The referee signals the start. Jacob doesn't move, but he

does narrow his reptilian eyes and flick his forked tongue between his lips. He lets his opponent advance, measuring his speed. Slow. So slow. It's almost boring.

The opponent throws a powerful right hook that would shatter concrete. Jacob isn't there to receive it. He's already behind the larger boy, his strike connecting with a point between the shoulders. The opponent staggers, off-balance. Jacob follows with three rapid hits—temple, kidney, back of knee. Clinical. Efficient. Devastating.

The match ends in twenty-six seconds.

Jacob returns to the warm-up area while the crowd's murmurs grow. He hears snippets:

"—never seen speed like—"

"—must be a Class Eight at least—"

"—barely saw him move—"

Master Han hands him a towel. Jacob doesn't need it. He hasn't broken a sweat.

The second match follows a similar pattern. Jacob's opponent is technically proficient, a traditional martial artist with years of disciplined training. It doesn't matter. Jacob moves between the spaces of the boy's techniques, finding openings that exist for microseconds, exploiting them before they close. The match lasts forty-three seconds.

Digital scoreboards flash his victories in rapid succession. The tournament officials confer in hushed tones, checking his nanite registration paperwork multiple times. Class 7 and above enhancements are allowed, but they've never seen implementation this seamless, this complete. Jacob pretends not to notice their suspicious glances.

In the VIP section, Master Han sits surrounded by his

betting partners. They no longer try to be subtle. Credit transfers flash between wrist devices after each of Jacob's matches. Han's expression never changes, but the satisfied tilt of his chin tells Jacob everything.

As Jacob prepares for his semi-final match, he catches a familiar face in the crowd. Kenji Park stands near the exit, arms crossed, watching intently. Their eyes meet briefly. Kenji doesn't smile or nod.

The semi-final opponent has a Class 6 agility enhancement—better, but still insufficient. Jacob dispatches him in fifty-two seconds. Not a single blow lands on Jacob's body. The referee raises his hand in victory while the crowd erupts.

The final match brings Jacob face-to-face with a previous champion—Zhang Wei, seventeen, with three regional titles to his name. He possesses a Class 7 combat suite, similar to Jacob's but with longer integration time. A true challenge at last.

They circle each other warily. Zhang attacks first, a blindingly fast combination that would overwhelm any normal fighter. Jacob blocks, counters, but his strike meets empty air. Zhang has already moved. *Shit.*

The crowd holds its collective breath. Jacob has no plans to lose.

Jacob becomes pure reaction, pure instinct. The match stretches to three minutes. Neither of them landing clean strikes. Then Jacob finds the pattern in Zhang's movements, a millisecond hesitation before his left kicks. Jacob zeroes in on it, times his counter perfectly. His fist connects with Zhang's solar plexus. The champion doubles over, his defense momentarily broken. Jacob doesn't hesitate. Three strikes in rapid succession.

Zhang hits the mat. Stays down.

Victory.

The arena erupts. Master Han's betting partners exchange triumphant looks. Officials approach with the championship medal and certificate. Cameras flash. Jacob stands at the center of it all, not tired, not even breathing hard. Already thinking of the next challenge, the next tournament, the next opponent to overcome. He smiles for the cameras. Gives them a show of his reptilian eyes and tongue. What else could he add?

In the locker room afterward, Jacob unwraps his hand bindings. The door opens. Kenji enters in street clothes.

"Impressive performance," Kenji says, leaning against the lockers. "The speed nanite suits you."

Jacob nods, not looking up. "Thanks. Didn't expect to see you here."

"Supporting a friend in the lower division." Kenji shrugs. "Plus I wanted to see if the rumors were true."

"What rumors?"

"That you've gone full enhancement. That Han's turning you into his personal cash machine."

Jacob knew the time would come when he would be challenged, but there's no accusation in Kenji's tone. They've become friendly over the last couple of years. "I'm winning. We're out of the shelter. My mom has a real job now. Seems like it's working out."

Kenji steps closer, lowering his voice. "Nanites are a slippery slope, man. And Han is even slipperier. I refused the last one and he's cancelled some of my tournaments."

Jacob wondered why Kenji hasn't been training as much. Now he knows.

"That's your choice," Jacob says, standing to face his friend. "This is mine."

"Is it? Or is it Han's?"

Jacob turns away, stuffing his gear into his bag. "He's my path to the top. My mother will never see another shelter again."

"At what cost?" Kenji asks softly. "Look at yourself, man."

Jacob's eyes find the mirror on the locker room wall. His reflection stares back—the eyes, the tongue, the tattoos. He's been thinking about adding a skin augmentation. A nanite that makes his skin glow golden and will leave an aura of golden light behind when he's using his speed.

He notes the improvements in the mirror. Enhanced reflexes. Enhanced speed. Enhanced Jacob. Improved Jacob. Better, stronger, faster Jacob.

But still Jacob?

"I know what I'm doing," he tells Kenji, zipping his bag closed. *I'm staying at the top.*

Kenji heads for the door, pausing with his hand on the handle. "They start as tools," he says. "Then they become crutches. Then they become you." He offers a sad smile. "Just be careful who's holding the leash when that happens."

CHAPTER 8

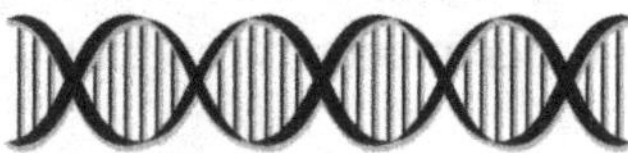

THE SMELL HITS Jacob before he opens his eyes. Butter and something sweet sizzling in a pan, the kind of breakfast he always craved when living at the shelter. *Pancakes.*

Jacob swings his feet to the floor. He pulls on a t-shirt and sweatpants, then follows the scent down the hallway, stopping at the kitchen doorway. His mother stands at the stove, her back to him, spatula in hand as she flips pancakes. The batter sizzles and pops, tiny specks spattering across the stove.

"You're making pancakes," Jacob says, leaning against the doorframe.

She turns, spatula raised. "Found the mix at that market on Seventh. The one with the blue awning." Her smile comes easier these days, stretches wider. "They had real maple syrup too."

Jacob watches her slide the spatula under a perfectly golden circle. She seems... happy.

"Sit," she says, gesturing with the spatula. "Before they get cold."

The table is already set with two mismatched plates on the scratched surface, forks that don't belong to the same set, a bottle of syrup that looks impossibly fancy compared to everything else they own. Jacob slides into his chair, watching as his mother places three fluffy pancakes on his plate.

She laughs at his expression. "Champions need fuel, right?"

"Right," he echoes, cutting into the stack. The first bite floods his mouth with sweetness. Nothing like the dry cereal bars from the shelter, or the dense protein shakes Master Han pushes during training.

His mother slides into the chair across from him. She pushes an envelope toward him, her fingers leaving a tiny smudge of flour on the crisp white paper. "This came yesterday. While you were training."

Jacob sets down his fork and picks up the envelope. The return address bears the logo of NanoBurst, one of the biggest supplement companies in the industry. He's seen their advertisements on the digi-boards downtown, featuring fighters with twice his reputation.

"They want to put your face on protein drinks," his mother says, cutting into her pancake. "The letter mentions a 'significant compensation package.'"

Jacob's fingers tighten around his fork. "How significant?"

She takes a sip of water. "More than I make in three months at the office."

The number hangs between them. Three months of

income for what, a photoshoot? His signature? The right to plaster his face across protein bottles?

"There'd be appearances," his mother continues. "Demos at stores. Social media obligations." She pauses. "Master Han already called to say he approves. Says it's good exposure."

Of course he does. Master Han gets seventy-five percent of everything. More exposure means more tournaments. More tournaments means more bets. More bets means more money for Han and his gambling friends.

"We could move somewhere better," Jacob suggests. "Buy something with our own money."

His mother reaches across the table and presses her palm against it, fingers splayed across the scratch marks.

"I love this place," she says. "I know it's not much, but it's not the shelter. And I don't want to forget where we came from. It's cozy. And I can hear you practicing in the dojo."

Jacob swallows. "But we could afford better now."

"We could," she agrees. "But I don't mind the paint. Or the sink that drips. Or the neighbor who plays accordion at midnight." She smiles. "They're our problems. Not the shelter's problems."

Jacob nods. After years of communal living, of rules and curfews and strangers' decisions controlling their lives, even a small apartment feels like a castle.

Still, he wants to give her more. She deserves more.

"I'll do the NanoBurst deal," he says, pulling the contract from the envelope.

"Only if you want to."

"I want to," Jacob says.

He doesn't mention the headache pounding behind his

right temple, the one that started three days ago after his last match and hasn't fully subsided. Doesn't mention how his hands sometimes shake when he isn't actively controlling them, or how he wakes up some nights with his heart racing for no reason. The speed nanite has side effects that Master Han never listed. But it doesn't matter. Jacob wouldn't change it for anything.

All he has to do is keep winning, and his mother will always have a roof over her head. Keep winning, and she doesn't return to double shifts and bleeding hands. Keep winning, and they stay out of the shelter system permanently.

He takes another bite of pancake. The sweetness now feels cloying against his tongue.

Another side effect he's noticed lately—a growing edginess when he's around too many altereds in one place. At tournaments, where enhanced fighters cluster in warm-up areas, his skin prickles with a strange electricity. His breathing gets shallow. His focus narrows to pinpoints of light.

But around unadjusteds, he feels calmer. Steadier.

The irony doesn't escape him. His body, pumped full of enhancements, craves normalcy while depending on abnormality to succeed.

"I'll call them today," his mother says, gathering their empty plates. "Set up the meeting."

Jacob nods. "More tournaments are coming up anyway. The Western Regional qualifiers next month. Then nationals if I place."

"*When* you place," his mother corrects.

Jacob smiles. "Right. When."

He watches her rinse the plates, humming softly to herself. Nothing is more important than winning. Than the nanites. Than being the best he can be.

Three days later, Jacob steps onto the sidewalk outside Master Han's dojo, the morning crowd already thick despite the early hour. His enhanced senses immediately catalog everything—temperature (seventy-two degrees), humidity (high), nearby conversations (fourteen distinct threads), traffic patterns (congested on the main avenue)—a constant stream of data he can't shut off. The nanites never sleep, even when he does. He's asked Kenji about it, but his friend doesn't experience the same side effects. Jacob did some research online. There are a whole range of reported side effects. At least he isn't experiencing the dry mouth and erectile dysfunction. Not that he has a girlfriend. Sensei Han keeps him too busy.

He adjusts his duffel bag strap and heads east toward downtown, where the buildings climb higher and the ads shine brighter. Three blocks from the dojo, the first digiboard flashes his image. Jacob freezes mid-stride. There he is, twenty feet tall, executing a spinning hook kick in ultra-high definition. The footage is from last month's tournament, the decisive moment when he defeated the regional champion. Below the image, bold text proclaims: "SportFuel: The Choice of Champions."

They didn't waste any time. The ink is barely dry on the contract and already his face dominates the skyline.

Jacob stares, transfixed. The boy on the screen doesn't look like him. Too polished. Too confident. Too... altered.

A couple walking past follows his gaze to the digi-board. The woman nudges her partner.

"That's him," she whispers. "The fighter. The one who took down Zhang Wei."

Jacob ducks his head and continues walking, but not before catching the man's impressed nod in his direction. The recognition sends a strange tingle up his spine. Not unpleasant. Just unfamiliar.

Another block, another digi-board. This time it's a still image—Jacob mid-punch, eyes locked on an opponent just out of frame. The caption reads: "Reflex. Speed. Power. SportFuel."

The neon hum of the advertisement pulses in time with the city's heartbeat. Blue and red and electric green, washing the morning commuters in artificial daylight. Each screen he passes shows some version of himself.

A group of kids huddled on a corner catches his attention. Four of them, none older than twelve, mimicking fighting stances with exaggerated grunts. One boy throws a wild roundhouse kick that nearly sends him tumbling into the street.

"No, like this," says another, demonstrating a more controlled version. "You gotta pivot on your back foot, like Jacob Shea does."

Jacob slows his pace, watching from the periphery. The youngest kid—skinny, with a mop of untamed curls—wears a white t-shirt with "JACOB SHEA" scrawled across it in permanent marker. A homemade tribute that makes Jacob's chest tighten.

The curly-haired kid spots him first. His eyes widen.

"Holy shit," he whispers. "It's him."

All four boys freeze like startled deer. Jacob considers walking past, pretending he didn't notice. But the naked admiration on their faces stops him.

"Your stance is pretty good," he tells the one who was correcting the others. "But you're telegraphing your kicks."

They stare at him, speechless. Then the curly-haired kid in the makeshift shirt thrusts a crumpled flyer into his hand.

"Can you sign this?" His voice cracks. "Please?"

The paper is a tournament announcement from three months ago, Jacob's name highlighted in a bold red. He takes it, suddenly aware of his own celebrity in a way the digi-boards couldn't convey.

"Does anyone have a pen?" he asks.

Four hands immediately thrust pens in his direction.

Jacob signs the flyer, then each boy's notebook or arm or, in one case, the back of a school ID card. They pepper him with questions about training and nanites and his signature kick. He answers what he can, surprised at how easily the words come.

"My brother says you're gonna be world champion," the curly-haired boy declares. "He says you're the fastest fighter he's ever seen."

Jacob smiles. "Tell your brother thanks."

"You're eyes are so cool, dude," says another.

Jacob flicks out his forked tongue to a squeal of appreciation.

"Good luck in the next tournament."

He continues downtown after extracting himself from

the impromptu fan club, their excited chatter following him half a block. He can't wipe the grin off his face.

Jacob passes three more digi-boards towering above the city streets. People point. Whisper. Some nod respectfully. One man even mimes a bow as Jacob passes.

Is this what Master Han promised? Not just tournaments and money, but this—recognition. Respect.

Jacob stops at a corner store, the same one he's visited weekly since moving to the neighborhood. Before the nanites, before the victories, it was one of the few places that extended him credit when money was tight. The bell above the door chimes as he enters.

The owner, a stout man with salt-and-pepper hair, glances up from his register. Recognition dawns across his face.

"Champion!" he booms, coming around the counter with outstretched arms. "I saw your fight last week. Incredible! My nephew recorded it for me."

Jacob accepts the man's enthusiastic handshake. "Just picking up some basics, Mr. Chen."

Mr. Chen waves dismissively. "Whatever you need. On the house."

"That's not necessary—"

"Champions don't pay here," Mr. Chen insists, already filling a bag with energy drinks from the refrigerated section. "Not in my store."

Jacob starts to protest again, but something in the man's expression stops him. There's pride there. Like he's somehow connected to Jacob's success, having witnessed his journey from the shelter kid who counted pennies for ramen to the face on the digi-boards.

"Thank you," Jacob says instead, accepting the bag.

Mr. Chen presses two extra energy drinks into Jacob's hands. "The blue ones. New formula. Good for recovery after training. Designed especially for people with speed nanites."

Jacob leaves the store with more than he came for. Six months ago, he was invisible. Now, he can't walk three blocks without seeing his own face. He wanted to be a fighter. The *best* fighter. He never considered the fame that went with it.

As he waits at a crosswalk, Jacob's phone buzzes. A text from Kenji: "Dude, you're blowing up! My whole timeline is Jacob Shea this, Jacob Shea that. Free drinks at the Hub tonight to celebrate?"

Jacob smiles, typing back: "I'm in. Bring whoever you want. It's on me."

He can do that now. Buy rounds for friends. Help out if Kenji needs anything. No more tight budgeting, no more choices between food and transportation, no more wearing the same three shirts until they fall apart. Clothing stores are falling over backwards and sending him free stuff. He now has more digi-tattoos than he can count—all complimentary. And instead of the golden skin nanite, he opted for something that makes his skin look slightly scaled to complete the reptilian look.

The walk signal changes. Jacob steps off the curb, still marveling at how quickly everything has changed. His face follows him across the intersection, projected from another digi-board on the corner.

Jacob pushes open the door to the apartment, balancing

three shopping bags in one arm, to find the living room transformed into a battlefield of cardboard boxes and plastic wrap. His mother kneels in the center, a power drill dangling from her hand, surrounded by pieces of what might eventually become a bookshelf. She looks up, blowing a strand of hair from her face, and grins. "The delivery guys came an hour ago. All at once."

He sets down the bags and surveys the chaos. Five large boxes lean against the far wall. A rolled carpet stands in the corner. Smaller packages litter every surface.

"I thought we were going to wait until the weekend," Jacob says, picking his way through the obstacle course of cardboard and foam packing material.

"The shelving unit was on backorder." His mother shrugs. "Then suddenly everything arrived together. Seemed like a sign."

Jacob crouches beside her, examining the instruction sheet spread on the floor. Diagrams with tiny arrows point to parts labeled in multiple languages. "Need help?"

She hands him the drill. "My wrist's getting tired."

They work in companionable silence, Jacob drilling pilot holes while his mother sorts screws into small piles according to size. When they stand the bookshelf upright against the wall, his mother steps back to admire their work.

"Perfect," she declares. "Now for the digi-board."

They tackle the living room wall next. Jacob mounts the bracket while his mother unpacks the thin screen that cost more than their monthly bills. A splurge, but one he insisted on when he saw her lingering over the display model in the electronics store.

"You remember how to program it?" Jacob asks as he tightens the final screw on the mount.

She gives him a look that manages to be both offended and amused. "I was programming interfaces before you were born." Her fingers dance across the setup panel as the screen flickers to life. "There."

The digi-board illuminates with a rotating gallery of martial arts legends. Bruce Lee in his iconic yellow jumpsuit. Mas Oyama breaking bricks with his bare hands. Modern champions in tournament rings. The images shift every thirty seconds, each fighter captured in a moment of perfect form.

Jacob stares at the display, a strange feeling settling in his chest. Someday his image might cycle through screens like this in other homes, other dojos.

They turn their attention to the stack of frames leaning against the couch. Each contains one of Jacob's tournament certificates, professionally matted and encased behind non-glare glass.

"I was thinking a grid pattern," his mother says, holding up her hands to frame the empty wall space beside the digi-board. "Three rows of three to start. Room to add more."

Jacob nods, measuring the wall with his eyes. His mother marks placements with pencil dots while Jacob follows with the drill, anchoring plastic wall plugs for the hanging wires. Each certificate finds its place in the growing display—regional qualifiers, championships, exhibition matches.

His mother unwraps the final frame, this one smaller than the others. Inside isn't a certificate but his first medal. The medal that started everything.

"This one goes in the center," she says. "Where everyone will see it first."

"But it's just bronze," Jacob protests. "From a minor tournament. I've won gold in bigger events since then."

His mother shakes her head. "This one matters most." She runs her finger along the medal's edge. "This one you won as just yourself."

Jacob wants to argue that he's still himself, nanites or no nanites, but the words stick in his throat. Instead, he takes the frame from her hands and centers it carefully in the middle of the grid, where it glints dully compared to the glossy certificates surrounding it.

They move to the kitchen next, applying a fresh coat of paint to cover the walls. Jacob moves the roller while his mother follows behind with a smaller brush, catching the edges and corners he misses.

"Hand me the tape?" Jacob asks, pointing to the blue painter's roll on the counter.

She tears off a strip and passes it to him. They slap strips of tape along the ceiling edge, step back together to check their work. Paint splatters their old clothes—his high school gym shirt, her faded cleaning uniform repurposed as DIY wear. White flecks dot his mother's hair like fallen stars.

By evening, the apartment is transformed. New shelves line the walls, filled with books they've collected over months of visiting discount stores. The digi-board cycles through fighting legends in the corner. The grid of certificates maps Jacob's journey from unknown to champion. Fresh paint brightens the kitchen, still drying in the soft glow of the new floor lamp.

His mother collapses onto their new sofa, an L-shape in dark blue they chose together online. Her eyes droop as she tucks her feet beneath her.

"Just resting my eyes for a minute," she murmurs. "Then we'll finish the kitchen."

Jacob nods, though he knows she won't last much longer. One minute stretches to five, then ten. Her head tilts against the cushion, hair falling across her face in a dark curtain.

He watches her for a moment. He would do anything for this woman. This selfless woman who fought to keep him safe and loved.

The blanket they purchased that morning still sits folded in its packaging. Jacob removes the plastic wrap, shakes out the soft fabric, and carefully drapes it over his mother. He tucks the edges around her shoulders.

"I'll finish the kitchen," he whispers.

Jacob finds the brush, and using his speed, completes the painting in a few minutes.

There are still paint flecks on his skin when he arrives at the dojo the next day. Jacob's bare feet squeak against the mat as he circles Kenji, both of them moving in a familiar dance. Kenji feints left, testing Jacob's defenses with a probing jab that doesn't commit. Jacob reads the intention before the movement completes. He parries easily, countering with a low kick that Kenji blocks with his shin.

"Getting predictable, Shea," Kenji says, bouncing lightly on the balls of his feet.

Around the training mat, younger students have paused their own practice to watch. Their faces reflect the same awe Jacob once felt watching from the sidelines, back when he was just the cleaner's son. Now he's the main attraction, the local champion whose tournament victories earn him whispers of respect even from Master Han's senior students.

The training droid hovers at the edge of the mat, its single camera eye tracking their movements, recording speed metrics and impact force for later analysis. Master Han insisted on the expensive equipment after Jacob's third tournament win. "To optimize your training," he'd said, though Jacob suspects it's more about optimizing Han's betting odds.

Jacob launches a combination—jab, cross, hook—flowing from one strike to the next. Kenji blocks the first two but has to duck the hook, his defensive movement a fraction slower than Jacob expects. They've sparred enough times that Jacob knows Kenji's rhythms intimately. There's something different today. Something... off.

"New gi?" Jacob asks, resetting his stance. "Seems stiffer than your old one."

Kenji grins. "Not the gi that's different."

Before Jacob can process the comment, Kenji explodes forward with a blinding combination. Left jab, right cross, spinning elbow—standard sequence, but the execution is anything but standard. The strikes come faster than they should, the final elbow catching Jacob in the ribs despite his enhanced reaction time.

Jacob stumbles back, more surprised than hurt. Kenji has never been able to land that cleanly on him, not since the nanites. Not since Jacob became something more than human.

The training droid beeps, registering the successful strike, its digital display flashing with updated metrics. Jacob narrows his eyes, reassessing his opponent.

"What did you do?" he asks, though he already suspects the answer.

Kenji rolls his shoulder. "Got a new nanite last week," he admits. "Realized I had to step up if I wanted to stay in the competition. It's speed enhancement. Only first generation, but it still works."

Jacob raises both brows. Kenji, who lectured Jacob about the dangers of enhancement, who warned him about becoming Master Han's "personal cash machine," has crossed the line he once drew so firmly in the sand.

"Congratulations," Jacob says, the word coming out more curtly than he intends.

A shadow flickers across Kenji's face. "You left me no choice. Everyone's chasing your records now. Regular training doesn't cut it anymore." He settles back into a fighting stance. "Not if you want to win."

They circle each other again, the dynamic between them shifting. For months, they've maintained the fiction that Jacob's enhancements don't matter, that their friendship exists separate from the competitive hierarchy of the dojo. But Kenji's admission has shattered that pretense.

"Let's see what you've got," Jacob says, tapping his guard up.

They engage again, this match more intense than before. Jacob pushes his reflexes to their limit, moving with the full capability the nanites allow. Kenji responds in kind, his newly enhanced speed making him a legitimate threat rather than just a sparring partner.

The beeping of the training droid accelerates as it struggles to keep pace with their movements. Jacob lands a spinning back kick that sends Kenji sliding across the mat. Kenji recovers with unnatural quickness, launching immediately into a combination that forces Jacob to give ground.

"Still not as fast as you," Kenji says between breaths, "but I'm catching up."

The words carry an edge that wasn't there before. This isn't just practice anymore. It's a statement. A challenge.

Jacob pushes forward, executing a complex sequence of strikes designed to overwhelm. Kenji meets each one, his defense adapting with each exchange, learning Jacob's patterns in real time. The first-generation speed nanite might not match Jacob's enhancements, but Kenji's natural talent narrows the gap.

"Master Han must be pleased," Jacob says, blocking a high kick. "Another winning fighter in his stable."

Kenji's expression hardens. "I didn't do this for Han. I did it for me."

"Sure," Jacob says, unable to keep the skepticism from his voice. "Just like I did it for me."

"You think I'm like you?" Kenji counters, his fist grazing Jacob's cheek. "Taking whatever Han offers without questioning?"

The comment stings more than the punch. Jacob retaliates with a sweep that catches Kenji off-balance, sending him to the mat. "You're taking more nanites now. Seems pretty similar from where I'm standing."

Kenji leaps to his feet in one fluid motion. "One additional nanite. On my terms. Not an entire suite that turns me into Han's property. Not reptilian eyes and scaled skin and digi-tattoos that cover my entire body."

"Those were my choices," Jacob snarls.

"It completes the look."

They close distance again, each strike carrying extra weight of unspoken accusations.

"At least I'm honest about what I am," Jacob says, landing a body shot that forces air from Kenji's lungs.

"Are you?" Kenji gasps, but recovers quickly. "You're on billboards all over the city. The face of SportFuel. The dojo's star. Are you being honest about the cost? How much is Han taking?"

Jacob falters for a split second, long enough for Kenji to slip past his guard with a right hook that connects solidly with his jaw.

The training droid beeps frantically, registering the clean hit. The watching students fall silent. No one lands hits on Jacob Shea anymore. Not since the nanites.

They separate, both breathing hard. Their eyes lock across the mat.

"Nice shot," Jacob concedes, touching his jaw.

Kenji nods, neither apologetic nor triumphant. "Same time tomorrow?"

Jacob resets his stance in answer. The training droid beeps once, signaling the continuation of the session. The younger students lean forward.

As they circle each other again, Jacob realizes this is just the beginning. Kenji with two nanites is dangerous. Kenji with more would be a genuine rival. Is that what he wants? Someone who can match him? Challenge him? Or is this the first crack in his downfall?

The thought vanishes as Kenji attacks again, and Jacob surrenders to the fight.

CHAPTER 9

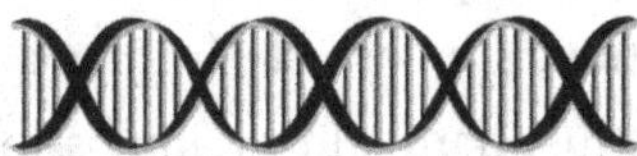

THE SILVER CASE sits on Master Han's desk. It's a small thing, but it seems to suck all the air out of the room. Jacob can't look away from it. Despite the money he's earned, he doesn't have enough to pay for this kind of nanite. And if he wants to stay at the top, he needs it.

Master Han circles his desk. His fingers slide across the polished wood surface, coming to rest on the case.

"Your victory in the East Coast qualifier was impressive," Han says. "But the World Championship requires something more."

Jacob sweats in the cool room. He's surprised that speed nanites don't come in built with an EverFresh element. But he can buy one of those from the drug store for $100.

"The Zhang rematch is coming up first."

"Zhang has upgraded." Han taps the case. "As have the others. Speed and reflexes are becoming... common."

Jacob has heard the whispers in locker rooms, seen the footage of other fighters moving faster, reacting quicker. The edge he once held is eroding with each tournament. Every week, more fighters show up with the same enhancements he pioneered.

Han flips the latch on the box.

"Class Ten," Han says as the lid rises. "Teleportation."

Jacon's mouth falls open. He's never met anyone with the skill of teleportation. On or off the mats. It's hard to get approved for. Not just hard, almost impossible. And it costs... more than he can comprehend.

His gaze drops to the pill. It's smaller than his previous nanites, a deep cobalt blue with a faint pulse of light at its core.

"How did you—" Jacob starts to ask, then stops himself. Some questions are better left unasked when it comes to Master Han's connections. The black market for high-class nanites is ruthlessly policed, but somehow Han always has access. Or maybe it's legit.

"This is beyond speed," Han continues. "Beyond reflexes. This is instantaneous repositioning. Displacement at will." His expression reveals a flicker of excitement. "You will be untouchable."

Jacob stares at the pulsing blue pill. *Class 10*. The highest classification available to civilians, and even then, only to the elite. The kind of enhancement that changes not just competitions but entire combat strategies. There are a few in the military, but not as many as you'd think. Can't have the soldiers going rogue.

"Side effects?" Jacob asks. Not that it matters. He already deals with headaches and bloody noses. He'll deal with whatever this pill gives him too.

"Initial disorientation. Some users report headaches during integration." Han dismisses the concerns with a wave, just as he did with the previous nanites. "Nothing a champion can't handle."

Jacob thinks of his mother waiting at home, of the apartment they've made into a home. Of the cooking classes she's started taking in her free time, now that she only works one job. Of the stack of college brochures on his desk.

He also thinks of Kenji's face during their last sparring session, the arguments they've been having about nanites. But neither of them have a choice. The entire dojo ecosystem is changing. Hell, the world is changing. More adjusteds every day. More abilities every week. The planet has become a playground for comic book superheroes.

Could he be a superhero? If he takes the teleportation nanite, he could fight crime. Prevent old ladies from being mugged in the streets. Prevent kids from being bullied at school. Bank robberies, rape, murder... he could use his abilities for more altruistic activities. But that's not going to put food on the table.

"The World Championship purse is two million," Han says. "Plus endorsements that could triple that. Your mother would never have to work again."

It always comes back to this. The carrot dangling just out of reach. First it was getting out of the shelter. Then it was a better job. Now it's complete financial security. The goalposts keep moving, but the game remains the same—take the nanite, win the match, collect the reward.

But he wants the title. More than anything.

"I'm in," Jacob says.

Han lifts the pill from its foam nest and extends it on his palm. An offering. No, not an offering. A contract.

Jacob's picks up the pill and slides it between his lips before he can change his mind.

For three heartbeats, nothing happens.

Then his skull cracks open.

Not literally, but that's how it feels. Like someone has taken a hammer to the back of his head and split him from crown to nape. Jacob gasps, grips the edge of the seat until his knuckles ache. The pain is immediate and overwhelming, radiating outward from the base of his skull in violent pulses.

"Breathe through it," Han instructs, his voice sounding distant. "Integration is more intense with higher classifications."

Jacob tries to nod, but the movement sends another spike of agony through his temples. The room blurs around him, colors smearing like wet paint. His vision tunnels, then expands beyond normal parameters. For a disorienting moment, he sees the office from multiple angles simultaneously—from where he sits, from the ceiling corner, from behind Han's desk.

The sensation of displacement intensifies. His body feels both heavy as stone and light as air. Something pulls at his center, like a hook embedded in his solar plexus trying to yank him in all directions at once.

"What's—" Jacob attempts, but his words slur together as another wave of pain crashes over him.

The room shifts. Or maybe he shifts. The distinction becomes meaningless as space itself seems to fold around him. Jacob blinks, and for a microsecond, he's standing by the window instead of sitting on the seat. Another blink, and he's back, the transition so swift he can't be sure it happened at all.

"Excellent," Han says, watching closely. "Your nervous system is adapting quickly. Just as I expected."

The pain begins to recede, fading from unbearable to merely excruciating. Jacob's breathing steadies as the room stops its nauseating spin. The strange perception of multiple viewpoints collapses back into normal vision. He becomes aware that he's drenched in sweat, his training shirt clinging to his back and chest.

"How do you feel?" Han asks.

"Like I died," Jacob manages, his voice hoarse. "Then came back wrong."

Han smiles. The bastard. "That's precisely what happened, in a manner of speaking. Death of limitations. Rebirth of possibility." He clasps his hands behind his back, surveying Jacob like a sculptor admiring his work. "The World Championship is no longer a goal. It's an inevitability."

Jacob closes his eyes, feeling the nanite settle into his system. The pain continues to ebb, replaced by a strange awareness of space—distances, dimensions, the gap between objects.

"Tomorrow," Han says, "we begin a new schedule."

Jacob nods, the movement no longer sending spikes of pain through his skull. The worst has passed. What remains is a dull throb and the unsettling sense that he's both entirely himself and something altogether different.

World Champion. The title echoes in his mind, drowning out the lingering discomfort.

✕✕✕✕✕✕

The arena lights beat down on Jacob like artificial suns, turning his skin slick with sweat before the match even begins. He bounces on his toes in the blue corner, feeling the mat give beneath his bare feet. The crowd is a living thing around him, twelve thousand people breathing and shifting and waiting for blood. Two months of training with the teleportation nanite and now this is his moment.

The announcer's voice booms across the space, introducing his opponent. "In the red corner, three-time national champion, the 'Enhancement Executioner'—Marcus Vega!"

The crowd roars as Vega enters the ring. He is six-foot-two of sculpted muscle and synthetic advantage. Jacob notes the visible enhancements: the unnatural blue sheen to Vega's eyes suggesting optical augmentation; the too-perfect symmetry of his musculature hinting at a Class 8 strength package; the fluid grace of his movement betraying at least one speed or reflex nanite.

Vega locks eyes with Jacob across the mat. There's no fear there. There should be.

"You know the drill," the referee says, bringing them to the center. "Clean fight. No strikes to the back of the head. Signal if you need to tap out." His eyes linger on Jacob a beat longer than necessary. He's seen the training videos. Everyone has.

The fighters touch gloves.

"Let's see what you've got, teleporter," Vega murmurs.

Jacob says nothing. Words are for before and after. Now is for action.

The referee steps back. "Fight!"

Vega advances immediately, cutting off the ring. His stance is reversed, right foot leading, body tilted forward. He's planning to rush him with a fast combo. It's a standard opening against a supposedly defensive fighter. Jacob has been labeled a counter-striker in all the analysis videos.

They don't know what he is now.

Jacob breathes deep, focusing on a point three feet behind Vega's left shoulder. The nanite activates at his intention, a warm pulse spreading outward from the base of his skull. The world compresses around him like he's being squeezed through a straw. Colors stretch and blur. His stomach lurches.

Then reality snaps back into focus.

He's behind Vega now, the transition instantaneous to observers but stretching into a surreal second for Jacob himself. Before Vega can register the disappearance, Jacob strikes—a perfect roundhouse kick to the kidney that lands with a meaty thud.

The crowd goes silent.

Vega stumbles forward, spinning to face the space where Jacob was, where Jacob should be. His eyes widen as he realizes what's happened.

The announcer's voice breaks the silence. "Did you... did you see that? Ladies and gentlemen, Jacob Shea just teleported! Literally vanished and reappeared!"

The crowd explodes, the noise a physical force. Jacob doesn't wait for Vega to recover. He focuses again, this time on a point above Vega. The compression sensation returns, briefer this time as his nerves disappear.

He materializes in mid-air, dropping onto Vega with a hammer fist that sends the larger fighter crashing to the mat. The impact shudders up Jacob's arm.

Vega rolls away. He throws a wild hook that cuts through empty air as Jacob teleports again, this time to Vega's right, striking with three rapid jabs to the temple.

"The Teleporting Terror!" the announcer screams into his microphone, coining a nickname. "This is unprecedented in competition fighting!"

Vega stumbles, his enhanced reflexes no match for an opponent who can simply disappear from in front of him. He attempts to grapple, lunging forward to clinch, but Jacob is gone before his arms can close. Reappearing behind him again, Jacob delivers a spinning back kick that folds Vega in half. He cannot keep the grin off his face. To take down someone with so many wins under his belt. There is nothing better.

The veteran fighter drops to his knees. The referee steps in, waving his arms to signal the end.

"Winner by technical knockout in forty-seven seconds —Jacob Shea!"

The timer on the massive display confirms it. It's the fastest victory in regional championship history. The previous record was two minutes, twelve seconds. Jacob has shattered it without taking a single hit.

Through the noise of the cheering crowd, Jacob spots Master Han at ringside, already on his phone. His face betrays nothing, but his rapid conversation and the gleam in his eyes tell Jacob everything. The bets have paid off. Handsomely.

Three men in expensive suits approach Han, business cards extended. New sponsors drawn by the spectacle.

Ignoring the blood running out of his nose from exertion, Jacob raises his arms as the referee presents him with the championship belt. This is what power feels like. Not just winning, but dominating.

Part of him misses the struggle, the test of skill against skill. But it won't be long before there are other teleporters in the circuit, so he's going to enjoy the winning streak while he can.

CHAPTER 10

ONE WEEK after the regional championship, Jacob stands in a smaller arena, the lights dimmer but the expectations infinitely higher. Everyone has seen the footage now. Everyone knows what he can do.

His opponent—a wiry fighter with lightning reflexes and fear in his eyes—circles the outer edge of the mat, keeping as much distance as possible. Smart. Useless.

Jacob concentrates on five points around the ring, mapping them in his mind. The referee signals the start. It's go time.

Jacob teleports to the first point directly behind his opponent. Before the man can turn, Jacob is gone again, materializing at point two, then three, then four, then five. Five displacements in under six seconds. With each transition, he lands a single strike—rib, kidney, temple, solar plexus, jaw. The final blow drops his opponent to the mat, unconscious before he hits the canvas.

The timer stops at seventeen seconds. A new record.

Hell, yes.

The crowd doesn't cheer so much as gasp collectively. The cameras struggle to track Jacob's movements, catching only blurs and afterimages. From the sidelines, Han raises a single approving eyebrow.

The announcer stammers through the victory declaration. Three different supplement companies approach Han before Jacob leaves the mat, contracts already drafted. The numbers have extra zeroes now.

"Dial it back next time," Han tells him in the locker room. "Give them a show. Twenty, thirty seconds at least. Makes for better footage."

Jacob nods, though he barely hears the instruction. His body buzzes with residual energy. Sleep will be difficult tonight. It always is now. Sometimes he wakes up in a park. Or the forest. Or in a random house he's never been to before. Thank God he never ends up too far from home. His teleportation only allows him to travel short distances. But he is dreading the day he gets stuck in the trunk of a tree.

The Eastern Invitational arrives two weeks later. A converted basketball arena with higher ceilings and theatrical lighting. Jacob's name on the marquee in letters twice the size of the other fighters'. Tickets sold out in eleven minutes. The betting pool is unprecedented for a non-championship event.

His opponent this time is a bulk. The man paces like a caged animal, eyes darting around the ring as if expecting Jacob to materialize at any moment. He's not wrong.

The bell rings. Jacob waits three full seconds, an eternity in fight time, before activating his teleportation. This time, he goes up. A new trick he's been working on that he's rather proud of.

Twenty feet above the mat, Jacob materializes near the ceiling rafters, clinging briefly to a support beam. The crowd gasps, thousands of faces turning upward in unison. His opponent spins, unable to locate him until someone in the front row points up.

Jacob lets go. He falls, focusing on a point directly behind his disoriented opponent. Mid-descent, he teleports again, appearing in perfect position for a rear choke hold. The fight ends with his opponent tapping frantically against his forearm, face purpling from lack of oxygen.

Twenty-eight seconds. Han nods approvingly from ringside.

The media explosion is immediate. "Defying Gravity" reads one headline. "Combat Evolution" claims another. Teleportation nanite applications triple nationwide in the week following the match, despite the astronomical cost and government restrictions.

Jacob wakes the next morning with dried blood on his pillow, a thin trail from his left nostril. He washes the evidence away before anyone can see it. The nosebleeds are becoming a regular thing, but it's all part of the process.

The sponsorship deals stack up on Han's desk. Protein supplements. Training gear. Exclusive gyms wanting his endorsement. A video game company negotiating for his likeness rights.

The numbers blur together. Jacob buys a flashy car. He goes on lots of dates, but he knows the girls are just there for the fame. He and his mother go house hunting. Maybe he'll get a dog. But Master Han insists they take over the other two floors above the dojo instead, so Jacob can be close to training. They put staircases in, and he gets an entire floor to himself.

One month later. The Southwest Championship. The largest venue yet, with broadcast rights sold to three different streaming platforms. Jacob's face on every screen in the building. The crowd chanting his name as he approaches the ring.

He is living the dream. How many shelter boys can say that?

His opponent is a veteran fighter with five different nanite enhancements, a walking arsenal of artificial advantages. The man shows no fear. Idiot. He's studied Jacob's previous matches, developed countermeasures. He believes he's prepared.

He isn't.

This time, Jacob teleports mid-strike. He throws a punch that starts in one location and connects from another, his fist seeming to disappear and reappear at the point of impact. He kicks from the left, vanishes, and completes the motion from the right. Physics becomes suggestion rather than law.

The veteran fighter backs away, defense crumbling. The victory takes twenty-four seconds. The arena erupts. Digital displays flash Jacob's name in ten-foot letters.

In the bathroom afterward, Jacob presses his forehead against the cool tile wall as a wave of dizziness washes over him. His vision tunnels briefly. When it passes, his nose is bleeding again. It's worse this time, a steady crimson stream that takes nearly five minutes to stop.

"Just fatigue," he mutters to his reflection. Maybe he'll buy himself a stamina nanite. "Just need more rest."

But rest is hard to come by. His schedule fills with appearances, demonstrations, photo shoots. The world wants to see the teleporter. Jacob complies, ignoring the headaches that follow each teleportation now, dismissing the moments when his vision doubles or his hands shake.

"You've adapted to the nanite faster than anyone I've seen," Han tells him after reviewing footage from the latest match. "Your neural pathways have fully integrated the displacement capabilities."

Jacob nods, swallowing a handful of painkillers when Han isn't looking. The persistent throb behind his eyes has become a companion, present even in quiet moments. He's waking up more often in strange places.

The victories come so easily now that they blur together in his memory. Seventeen seconds. Twenty-two seconds. Nineteen seconds. The names and faces of his opponents fade, irrelevant to the spectacle. What matters is the teleportation, each match a new opportunity to push the boundaries, to disappear and reappear in increasingly dramatic ways.

The crowd doesn't come to see a fight anymore. They come to see Jacob Shea defy reality.

On a rare evening when Jacob finds himself at a lose end, he takes his mother into the city for ice cream.

"Are you sure you're feeling okay?" his mother asks.

"Never better." Jacob forces a smile.

"I think you're right about buying our own place. It doesn't have to be far away."

"I'll think about it." Jacob has reached the stage where the successes have mounted up so dramatically that they are too good to be true. He's afraid to make a decision. Any decision.

Relies on Master Han's advice more than ever. He shouldn't, but he can't seem to help himself.

"You could build a training room in the basement."

Jacob wipes his nose to see his hand come back smeared with blood. He shoves his hand in his pocket before his mom notices.

"Maybe a hot tub too," his mom says. "So you can relax all those muscles after a fight."

Jacob raises an eyebrow. "Not much muscle usage going on in a twenty second fight."

His mom frowns. "No, but it must be tiring all the same. I hear nanites are tiring. They can wear you out. The speed, your metabolism..." she trails off with a sigh.

Jacob wraps an arm around her shoulder. "I'm all good, Ma."

She pats his hand and they discuss which ice cream flavors they're going to choose.

There is a buzz of activity as they approach downtown. In the main plaza, an installation crew swing a massive frame into position, hydraulic lifts whining under the weight.

"Is that what I think it is?" Jacob's mom asks.

Jacob gapes at the fifty-foot holo-poster as it rises against the glass face of Summit Tower. "I think so."

Traffic slows. Pedestrians stop mid-stride. Phones lift in unison, capturing the moment when Jacob's image claims another piece of the skyline.

A crowd forms, gathering in a loose semicircle beneath the installation. Most are teenagers, backpacks slung over shoulders, school uniforms rumpled from a day of confinement. They tilt their heads back, mouths slightly open, watching the technicians make final adjustments to the mounting brackets.

"That's gotta be the biggest one yet," says a lanky boy with a shock of red hair. "Bigger than the one by the transit station."

· His friend, shorter but broader across the shoulders, nods without lowering his phone. "SportFuel's going all in on Shea. My dad says they've doubled their stock price since signing him."

A girl with intricate braids and a martial arts academy patch on her jacket pushes to the front of the growing crowd. "They're activating it," she calls back to her friends. "Look!"

The technicians flip a series of switches on the control panel. The image flickers once, twice, then bursts into life. Jacob Shea hovers above the plaza, frozen in mid-teleport. His body is partially transparent, a trail of blue energy marking the space between his departure and arrival points.

"Holy shit," breathes the red-haired boy. "It looks so real."

It does. The holographic technology captures every detail —the beads of sweat on Jacob's forehead, the tension in his muscles, the slight blur of movement around his edges, the fork of his tongue and the slit of his eyes.

The lead technician makes a final adjustment, and the poster's animation feature activates. Now Jacob cycles through a sequence of teleportations, his form dissolving into blue light before reappearing elsewhere on the display. The effect is hypnotic. The crowd gasps collectively as virtual Jacob blinks from one side of the poster to the other, leaving trails of energy in his wake.

"I'm definitely getting a teleportation nanite," announces

a younger boy, maybe fourteen. He wears a knockoff version of Jacob's competition uniform, the lightning bolt emblem slightly off-center. "My brother knows someone who can get Class Eights without government registration."

"You can't even afford a Class Two," scoffs an older teen. "Besides, teleportation's a Ten. Military and elite athletes only."

"For now," the younger boy insists. "Prices always drop. Remember when strength enhancements were just for billionaires? Now half my gym class has them."

The crowd swells as office workers flow out of the buildings, many wearing the branded SportFuel shirts that have become ubiquitous since Jacob's teleportation debut. Some carry the energy drinks with his silhouette on the label. A few wear the holographic wristbands that project a miniature version of Jacob performing his signature moves.

"I never thought it would be like this," Jacob's mother whispers to him.

"Me neither," Jacob replies.

His mom pats his hand. "You should find a nice girl."

"I'm seventeen."

"Exactly."

He rolls his eyes. If only his mom knew how hard it was to find someone who sees him for who he really is.

Who is he? Really? Jacob's not sure he knows the answer. He's certainly not the shelter boy anymore. And he never wanted to be anyone's puppet. But here he is.

"My cousin saw him at the mall last week," says a girl with purple-tinted glasses. "Said he teleported from the food court to the second level just because a kid asked him to. Didn't even charge for the demonstration."

"Bullshit," her friend replies. "He's got appearance fees. Nobody does that for free."

"Jacob would," insists a boy wearing a competition team jacket. "He came from nothing, you know. Lived in a shelter. Cleaned mats at his dojo before he could afford to train there."

The crowd murmurs with this piece of Jacob's mythology. His origin story has become as much a part of his brand as the teleportation. The shelter kid who rose to become the most recognizable fighter in the world. Rags to riches through nanite enhancement, the new American dream.

The holographic Jacob completes another teleportation sequence. This time he appears to leap through the poster's frame, seeming to materialize partly in the real world before being pulled back into the display. It's an illusion, but so convincing that several onlookers step back.

"Think it hurts?" asks the younger boy in the knockoff uniform. "Teleporting, I mean."

"Nah," says his friend confidently. "He'd show it if it did. Besides, nanites fix that stuff. My dad got a regen one for his back, and he says it's like being twenty again."

A sleek black car glides to the curb, its windows tinted. A woman in a sharp business suit emerges, surveying the installation. The SportFuel logo gleams on her tablet case.

"Perfect placement," she says into her earpiece. "Visibility from five major thoroughfares, pedestrian count averaging nine thousand per hour during peak times." She glances at the gathered crowd, the corners of her mouth lifting slightly. "Demographics skewing younger than projected. Primary target engagement already exceeding expectations."

The teenagers ignore her, too captivated by the holographic spectacle to notice they're being analyzed as market segments. The animated Jacob continues his sequence of moves across the massive display, appearing and disappearing in bursts of blue energy.

"There's another one going up by Central Station tomorrow," the red-haired boy informs his friends. "And they're replacing all the transit shelter ads with interactive ones where you can take a picture that makes it look like you're teleporting too."

The city is being remade in Jacob's image, one advertisement at a time. His face watches from buildings, buses, billboards. The ethereal blue glow of his teleportation effect has become SportFuel's signature color, appearing on everything from vending machines to the lights illuminating downtown skyscrapers at night.

"My coach says teleportation will be standard in competition within five years," says the girl with the martial arts patch. "Everyone will need it just to qualify for regionals."

"That's the point," replies an older teen who has remained quiet until now. He gestures toward the holographic poster with a cynical tilt to his mouth. "Show us something impossible, make us want it, then sell it to us at premium prices. Tale as old as time."

Jacob's stomach tightens at the words, but the other kids don't seem affected. For them, Jacob isn't selling anything, he's showing what's possible. He's redefining the boundaries of human potential. He's proving that someone from nowhere can touch the stars.

As the technicians complete their work and the crowd begins to disperse, the younger boy in the knockoff uniform lingers, still staring up at the holographic Jacob with naked admiration.

"Someday," he whispers to himself. "Someday that'll be me."

Above him, Jacob Shea teleports again and again in an endless loop.

CHAPTER 11

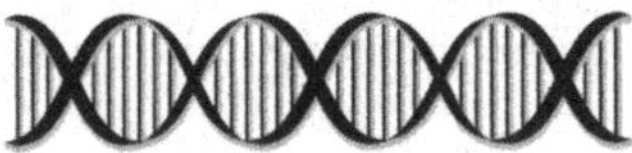

THE HALLWAY STRETCHES before Jacob like a tunnel, narrow and dim despite the victory lights still flashing in the arena behind him.

Another win.

Thirty-one seconds this time. He allowed his opponent to land one strike before ending it with a sequence of teleports that left the crowd screaming and the medical team rushing in to attend to his disoriented opponent.

A figure steps out from a doorway ahead, blocking the path to the locker rooms.

Kenji.

Jacob hasn't spoken to him in weeks, not since their last sparring session when Jacob accidentally teleported mid-match, disappearing from a hold that should have been inescapable.

"Nice performance," Kenji says.

The hallway narrows here, barely wide enough for two people to pass without touching. The overhead lights flicker, creating alternating patterns of shadow and sickly fluorescence across Kenji's face.

Jacob stops, maintaining ten feet of distance between them. "Thanks." He shifts his gear bag to his other shoulder. "Didn't know you were here."

"Wasn't planning to be." Kenji doesn't move from his position. "Got a call from someone who was concerned about you."

"My mother?" Jacob asks, though he already knows it wasn't her. She's stopped coming to his matches, claiming the crowds make her anxious.

Kenji shakes his head. "A referee from the Eastside tournament. Said you had a nosebleed after your match. Said your eyes didn't focus right during the post-fight interview."

Jacob tenses. He'd thought he'd handled that discreetly, stepping away from the cameras before the bleeding started, blaming the disorientation on dehydration. "I'm fine."

"Nanites have side effects," Kenji says, taking a step forward. "You need to stop letting Han use you."

"You don't know what you're talking about," Jacob says, fisting a hand. "Everyone in the circuit is taking nanites. It's normal."

"Normal?" Kenji's laugh is sharp, humorless. "Nothing about this is normal."

The roar of the crowd filters down the hallway. Someone else has won their match.

"I'm giving them what they want," Jacob says. "You've seen the crowds. The sponsors. People love it."

"People loved public executions once too." Kenji steps

closer. "Han's turned you into a circus act, and you don't even see it."

Jacob bristles. "I see everything just fine. I see my mother working a real job, living in a real home. I see college scholarship offers. I see a future that wouldn't exist if I was still throwing traditional punches and kicks like everyone else."

"At what cost, Jacob?" Kenji's voice softens. "When's the last time you went a day without a headache? When's the last time you slept through the night without teleporting involuntarily?"

Jacob starts. "How did you—"

"Han's last three teleporters burned out within a year," Kenji interrupts. "One had a stroke during a match. Another developed seizures. The third just disappeared. Literally. Never reconstituted properly during a teleport."

Jacob's skull throbs, a warning or an affirmation, he isn't sure. "You're making that up."

"Check the records. They're buried under non-disclosure agreements, but they exist." Kenji leans against the wall, suddenly looking tired. "Why do you think he's pushing you so hard? He needs to maximize his return before you break down too."

Jacob's throat tightens. He thinks of Han's insistence on more matches, more appearances, more demonstrations. The increasingly complex teleportation sequences he's asked to perform.

"I'm stronger than they were. Han says my DNA bonds exceptionally well," Jacob says.

"Maybe." Kenji straightens. "Or maybe you're just the next lab rat."

Anger flares hot in Jacob's chest. "That's rich coming from you. You have nanites too. You're just as enhanced as I was before teleportation."

"There's a difference between taking a reasonable enhancement and becoming a different species," Kenji counters, throwing a hand in Jacob's direction. "All that reptilian DNA? Are you even human anymore? You've crossed a line, Jacob. And Han is dragging you further across it every day."

"Han is using you too," Jacob snaps. "You think those tournaments you win are just about your talent? He's betting on you just like he bets on me."

A flash of something—hurt, maybe—crosses Kenji's face. "I know exactly what Han is doing. That's the difference. I keep my enhancements minimal. I maintain control of my career. I don't let him turn me into a product. And I don't let him take seventy-five percent."

Jacob blanches, struggles to breathe. Too much truth rings from Kenji's words. "You're a hypocrite. You criticized me for taking nanites, then got them yourself. You talk about maintaining control, but you still let Han manage your career. The only difference is I'm winning bigger than you ever will. And twenty-five percent of two mil is a hell of a lot of money."

Kenji's eyes narrow. "Is that what you think this is about? Jealousy?"

"Isn't it?" Jacob takes a step forward. "I'm doing what we all dreamed of as kids. I'm becoming legendary. Breaking records. Changing the sport forever."

"You're not changing the sport," Kenji says quietly. "You're destroying it. You're making it impossible for anyone without a Class Ten nanite to compete. You're creating an arms race that most fighters can't afford to join."

The accusation thickens the air between them. Jacob wants to dismiss it, but he's seen the desperation in his opponents' eyes. The way they take increasingly dangerous enhancement combinations trying to counter his teleportation. The injuries that result when their bodies reject the conflicting nanites.

"It'll be you next," Jacob says. "Han already has you on two nanites. How long before he suggests something more exotic? How long before you're standing where I am?"

Kenji shakes his head. "That's not going to happen. I've drawn my line."

"Everyone has a price," Jacob says.

"Do they?" Kenji steps aside, no longer blocking the path. "I guess we'll find out. Because I'm not walking your path, and deep down, I think you know you shouldn't be either."

Jacob moves past him, their shoulders almost brushing in the narrow space. He stops when they're side by side, not looking at each other. "I'll drop out of the circuit then," he says suddenly. "If you think it's so destructive."

He doesn't mean it. Not really. But some part of him wants Kenji to talk him down, to give him permission to continue.

Kenji doesn't take the bait. "No, you won't," he says softly. "You're in too deep now. The teleportation, the fame, the money... they've become who you are." He starts walking away. "Just remember who you were when things start falling apart."

Jacob stands frozen in the hallway, listening to Kenji's footsteps fade.

After a minute, he forces himself forward. He pushes the locker room door open. Inside, reporters wait with cameras and microphones. Sponsors with new contracts. Fans with smartphones ready to capture him on film.

The familiar rush returns—the adoration, the attention, the respect that comes with being untouchable. It washes away his doubts, drowns out the whispers of warning.

CHAPTER 12

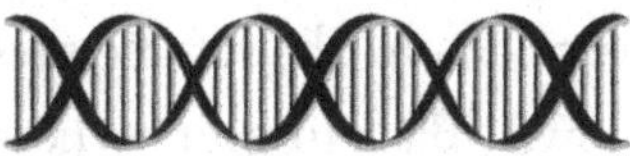

Twenty thousand people surround Jacob. Here. In this arena. Just to watch him. He can't help the smile stretch across his face.

His opponent is a muscular fighter with calculating eyes and three nanites documented in the pre-fight briefing: reflexes, strength, and pain suppression. A dangerous combination. But not dangerous enough.

Jacob inhales. Exhales. The crowd's roar fades to white noise as the referee steps between them.

National championship.

The words thrum through his body like a second pulse.

His opponent, Damon Lynch, bounces on the balls of his feet, muscles coiled beneath skin that gleams under the spotlights.

Jacob rolls his shoulders, loosening the tension. Across the arena, Master Han sits ringside, surrounded by men in suits worth more than Jacob's first tournament prize. Their faces glow with the blue light of wrist devices, numbers scrolling as bets are placed and adjusted. Jacob catches Han's eye. The slight nod. The unspoken command.

Win. At any cost.

No problem.

The referee signals them to the center. Lynch tracks Jacob's movements.

"Clean fight, gentlemen," the referee says, his voice nearly drowned by the crowd. "Back to your corners."

Jacob retreats. The countdown clock flashes on massive screens. Ten seconds until the fight begins. The crowd's chant builds—"Te-le-port! Te-le-port!"—a rhythmic demand for spectacle.

Five seconds.

Jacob focuses on his breathing. In through the nose, out through the mouth. The nanite hums beneath his skin, ready to tear him apart and reassemble him elsewhere. Ready to win him another title.

The buzzer sounds.

Lynch charges, closing the distance with frightening speed. A feint with his right, followed by a lightning-fast kick aimed at Jacob's ribs. Jacob sidesteps, the kick grazing his side with enough force to remind him why Lynch is in the final.

No more playing around.

Jacob activates the teleport, focusing on a point three feet behind Lynch. The world compresses, his vision tunneling as his body dissolves. For a fraction of a second, he is suspended in no man's land. Then reality snaps back, and he materializes behind his opponent.

Lynch spins, but too late. Jacob's strike connects with the

side of his neck, targeted at the cluster of nerves beneath the jaw. Lynch staggers, momentarily disoriented.

The crowd erupts.

No time to celebrate.

Jacob doesn't wait. He teleports again, this time to Lynch's left, landing a kidney shot that would drop most fighters. Lynch absorbs it, his pain suppression nanite earning its keep. He counters with a wild haymaker that cuts through empty air as Jacob disappears again.

Three teleports in under ten seconds. Sweat beads on Jacob's forehead, rolling into his eyes. The strain builds with each transition. His lungs burn as if he's been running for miles. The nanite demands energy, consuming his reserves with each displacement. But *hot damn* is it worth it.

Lynch adapts quickly. He begins anticipating, throwing strikes not where Jacob is, but where he's likely to appear.

Jacob materializes after his fourth teleport to find Lynch already pivoting toward him, a roundhouse kick scything through the air. He ducks, the kick whistling over his head, and counters with an uppercut that snaps Lynch's head back.

Still not enough.

The clock shows two minutes elapsed. Jacob's breathing comes harder now, each teleport leaving him more drained than the last. A faint metallic taste touches his tongue. Blood. From his nose or inside his mouth, he can't tell. Doesn't matter. *Keep going.*

He darts in with traditional strikes, saving the teleportation for critical moments. Jab, cross, hook. Lynch blocks the combination, his strength allowing him to absorb impacts that would stagger others. He counters with a flurry of his own, forcing Jacob back toward the edge of the mat.

Jacob feels it coming before he sees it—the sweep aimed at his legs. Lynch drops low, his leg extending in a move designed to take Jacob's feet from under him. A millisecond before contact, Jacob teleports.

This time, the displacement feels wrong. His reassembly comes with a wave of dizziness, the arena tilting sideways for a terrifying moment. He staggers upon materialization, nearly falling.

Lynch seizes the opportunity, charging forward with a flying knee aimed at Jacob's chest. The crowd's roar intensifies.

Not now. Not after everything.

Jacob steadies himself and focuses through the pain. One more teleport. He picks a spot directly above Lynch near the ceiling lights. The compression comes, followed by the void, then the snap back to reality. He materializes ten feet above the mat, gravity immediately reclaiming him.

He falls. Lynch looks up too late, eyes widening as Jacob descends toward him. Jacob teleports once more mid-air, reappearing behind Lynch as the fighter raises his arms to block the attack from above.

Perfect misdirection. If martial arts ever fail him, he could find a second career as a magician.

Jacob's spinning back kick connects with the back of Lynch's knee. The joint buckles. Lynch drops to one knee, momentarily defenseless. Jacob follows through with a vicious elbow to the temple that sends Lynch sprawling face-first onto the mat.

The referee jumps between them, waving his arms. "Stop! Fight's over!"

Jacob is panting, but it doesn't stop him grinning.

The referee grabs his wrist, lifting it high. "Winner by knockout and NEW National Champion, Jacob Shea!"

The crowd explodes, a wall of sound that slams into Jacob. His name echoes around the arena, chanted by twenty thousand voices. Confetti rains from the ceiling, catching in his sweat-soaked hair.

This is what it's all about.

Master Han stands with the sponsors, accepting handshakes and backslaps

Jacob turns in a slow circle, absorbing the moment. National Champion. The title he's dreamed of since that first day cleaning mats at the dojo. Only Worlds remain.

The medical team approaches, concerned by the blood now visibly trickling from his left nostril. Jacob waves them off with a practiced smile. "I'm fine," he says. "Lynch caught my nose."

The championship belt is brought into the ring, gold and leather gleaming under the lights.

The crowd continues its rhythmic chant: "Te-le-port! Te-le-port!"

Jacob raises his fists in acknowledgment as he is escorted to the podium.

Lights flash. Cameras click. The crowd's adoration washes over him.

The national anthem plays. Jacob places his hand over his heart. The blood has stopped flowing from his nose, but the metallic taste lingers on his tongue.

The federation president drapes a ceremonial robe over Jacob's shoulders, embroidered with the names of past champions.

"Ladies and gentlemen," the announcer's voice booms. "Your new National Champion, Jacob Shea!"

When the cheering subsides, he steps down from the podium.

Master Han materializes at his side.

"Excellent performance," Han says. "The sponsors are ecstatic."

Jacob nods, searching Han's face for some acknowledgment of the achievement itself, not just its marketability. He finds nothing but calculation behind the congratulatory smile.

"We rest for two weeks," Han continues as they walk toward the tunnel that leads to the locker rooms. "Then we begin preparation for Worlds."

Worlds. The ultimate stage. Fighters with enhancements that make Jacob's teleportation seem like a parlor trick. Neural acceleration suites. Military-grade reflexes. Combinations of nanites that push the boundaries of what human bodies can endure.

"The delegation from SportFuel wants exclusivity for the Worlds campaign," Han says. His eyes flick to his wrist device, scrolling through offers. "They're prepared to triple your current arrangement."

Jacob forces himself to focus on Han's words through the ringing in his ears. "Triple?"

Han nods, a rare smile creasing his face. "Your mother never needs to work again."

The words land where Han intended. Jacob's entire career, every enhancement, every risk—all of it circling back to that one goal. Security. Stability.

Han gives Jacob's shoulder a final squeeze. "The world wants more of the teleporter," he says. "We'll give them what they want."

The locker room offers a temporary sanctuary. Jacob sits on a bench. He removes the medal from around his neck, studies the weight of it in his palm. National Champion. The title that once seemed like an impossible dream.

The door bursts open. Jacob jumps to his feet. But it's not reporters or sponsors or medical staff.

It's his mother.

She rushes across the room, her face streaked with mascara tears. She throws her arms around him.

"You did it, baby!" she cries, her voice breaking. "I always knew you would."

Jacob enfolds her in his arms, burying his face in her hair to hide his own tears.

"I saw it all," she says, pulling back to look at his face. "The way you moved. It was beautiful. Like dancing."

She doesn't mention the blood she must have seen on the monitors, or the moment he staggered after a teleport.

She brushes his hair back from his forehead, a gesture unchanged since his childhood. "Your grandfather would be so proud. A champion in the family."

The door opens again. Han returns with sponsors in tow. Jacob watches his mother straighten her shoulders, smooth her department store dress.

"Ms. Shea," one of the sponsors greets her. "Your son has quite a future ahead of him."

His mom nods, her smile tight but proud. "He always has."

Han claps his hands together. "The press is waiting. Jacob, they want photos with the belt and medal."

Jacob stands, slipping the medal back around his neck, securing the championship belt at his waist.

"We've arranged a small celebration," Han continues. "At your new home. The sponsors insist."

Her eyes light up. "I should get home and prepare—"

"Already taken care of," Han interrupts smoothly. "Everything has been arranged. You just need to enjoy your son's success."

"Of course," she says. "Thank you."

After an hour of fielding questions, Jacob arrives at the home he and his mother moved into last week. But he barely recognizes the three-bedroom home. The moving boxes are gone, replaced by gleaming furniture he's never seen before. The walls display SportFuel's signature blue lighting. Caterers in crisp uniforms glide through spaces that still felt empty this morning. Han's doing. Of course.

"What happened to our stuff?" His mom whispers, her hand tightening around Jacob's arm.

Before he can answer, Han materializes beside them, champagne flute in hand. "Welcome home, champions," he says, the plural including his mother in a way he never has before. "I took the liberty of expediting your move-in process."

"Our things—" she begins.

"All carefully preserved," Han assures her. "The personal

items are in the master bedroom. The rest has been... upgraded."

Jacob surveys the space that was supposed to be theirs. The living room now features a wraparound sofa in butter-soft leather. A cutting-edge digi-wall displays his championship match on a loop, his teleporting form throwing that final, devastating blow again and again. Corporate logos float discreetly in the corners of each projection.

A table along one wall overflows with gifts. Training gear from SportFuel. A custom gi with his name embroidered in gold thread. A scale model of the World Championship arena where he'll compete next. A holographic training simulator worth more than their entire shelter dormitory.

"Your mother mentioned you wanted a dog," Han says, gesturing toward the backyard. "There's a breeder waiting on your call. Any breed. Any price point."

"This is too much," his mother says.

Han waves away her protest. "Nothing is too much for the family of our national champion."

The house fills with people. Sponsors in tailored suits. Federation officials with practiced smiles. Media personalities who compliment and flatter.

A sponsor claps Jacob on the shoulder, drawing his attention to the digi-wall. "Look at that teleport sequence," the man says, his voice thick with admiration or maybe just alcohol. "Never seen anything like it. The ratings were astronomical."

On screen, Jacob dissolves into blue light, reappearing behind his opponent in a move that seems to defy physics. The crowd roars. The opponent falls. Jacob's arms rise in victory.

Man, that felt good.

"We're rolling out the new campaign tomorrow," another sponsor says, joining them. "Your face on every transit hub in the country by noon. The teleporting champion, hero to a generation of enhanced athletes."

Jacob nods, accepting their praise while his temples throb with the beginning of a headache. Six teleports during the fight. More than he's ever attempted in such rapid succession. His body still hasn't fully recovered.

He excuses himself, slipping through the crowd toward the kitchen. The caterers have set up a makeshift bar there. Jacob asks for water, downing it in three long gulps. The cool liquid soothes his parched throat but does nothing for the pressure building behind his eyes.

"Looking for something stronger?" a voice asks.

Jacob turns to find a man he doesn't recognize. Judging by the SportFuel pin on his lapel, he's another sponsor.

"Just hydrating," Jacob replies.

The man nods. "Smart. Teleportation dehydrates like crazy. One of the lesser-known side effects." He extends his hand. "Dr. Warren. I consult for SportFuel's enhancement division."

Jacob shakes the offered hand, suddenly alert. "You work with teleportation nanites?"

"Among others." Dr. Warren studies Jacob with clinical interest. "You're integrating remarkably well. Most subjects experience significant displacement sickness after multiple teleports."

Subjects. Not fighters. Not athletes. *Subjects.*

"I get headaches," Jacob admits, unsure why he's confiding in this stranger. "And sometimes nosebleeds."

Dr. Warren nods. "Expected with a Class Ten. Nothing to worry about if they resolve quickly." His gaze sharpens. "They do resolve, yes?"

Before Jacob can answer, Han appears at his elbow. "Dr. Warren, I see you've met our champion." Han's tone is pleasant, but his eyes flash a warning. "Jacob, they're asking for you in the living room."

Jacob allows himself to be steered away, the doctor's question hanging unanswered between them. Do the symptoms resolve? Sometimes. Not always. Not lately. But does it matter when he's winning titles?

In the living room, Han raises his glass. The crowd falls silent.

"To Jacob Shea," Han announces. "National Champion today. World Champion tomorrow."

The guests echo the toast, glasses raising in unison. "To Jacob!"

The celebration continues into the night. Eventually, the crowd thins. Sponsors leave with promises of contracts to follow. Han departs last, his final instructions to Jacob clear: rest for a week, then back to training.

When the door closes behind the final guest, silence falls over the house. Jacob moves through the unfamiliar space, turning off lights, studying the furnishings that strangers selected for them. Everything is perfect. Expensive. Impersonal.

He stops at the window overlooking the city. Lights

twinkle across the urban landscape, some of them undoubtedly illuminating his image on billboards and digi-displays.

His mother's reflection appears beside his own as she joins him at the window. She's changed into her old robe, the one possession she insisted on keeping through every shelter move, every hardship. It's worn at the elbows, faded from too many washes, but she won't give it up.

"Are you okay?"

Jacob doesn't know how to answer that.

"Because if you're not, we'll find another way."

Jacob contemplates different paths. But Han will never let him go. And he wants Worlds. He really does. "Worlds is waiting for me."

His mother nods, then kisses his cheek. "You must be exhausted. Get some sleep."

Jacob follows her advice and crawls into bed. But a warning whispers at the back of his mind, and it sounds surprisingly like Kenji's voice.

CHAPTER 13

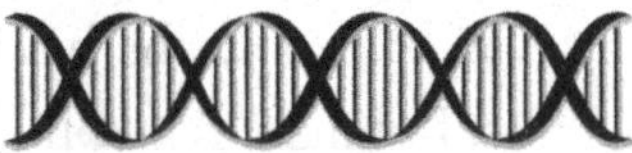

THE TELEPORT TEARS Jacob apart and reassembles him three feet to the left. His molecules scream in protest. This is the fourth transition in as many minutes.

His vision swims. Jacob staggers, catches himself before his knee can touch the mat.

"Again," Han commands from the shadows of the dojo.

Jacob's chest heaves. Sweat drips from his chin, pattering onto the mat. He focuses on a point near the ceiling, summoning the familiar burn of the nanite activating along his spine. The world compresses, stretches, tears—

He materializes six feet up and immediately falls, his ankle twisting as he lands. Pain shoots up his leg, white-hot and electric. He grits his teeth, tastes copper on his tongue.

"Sloppy," Han says, stepping into the light. "World champions don't stumble."

Jacob straightens, ignoring the throb in his ankle. "I need more recovery time between jumps."

"Your opponents won't give you recovery time." Han

circles him. "Zhang has upgraded to a Class Nine reflex package. Diaz has a new neural acceleration suite. They're training sixteen hours a day."

"I'm training eighteen," Jacob counters, wiping blood from his upper lip. Another nosebleed. The third today.

Han's eyes narrow. "And still falling short of the mark."

Jacob knows he is right. Knows he has to push harder if he wants to win Worlds. But man, is it killing him.

"Your teleportation is perfect," Han continues. "But your stamina is failing. The body wasn't designed for molecular displacement. It drains your reserves."

No shit. Each teleport feels like running a sprint. Six in succession leaves him gasping. Twelve brings the tremors in his hands that he hides in the pockets of his gi. Twenty... he hasn't managed twelve yet without passing out.

Han reaches into his pocket and produces a small metal case. It opens with a soft click. Inside lies a pill the color of sunset. It pulses with orange-red light, like an ember refusing to die.

"Stamina enhancement," Han says. "Class Eight. Military-grade. It recalibrates your cellular energy production. You'll teleport twenty times without fatigue."

Jacob stares at the pill. Stamina is something he is in desperate need of. He won't win without it.

"It's been specifically constructed for you. Based on your DNA and previous enhancements," Han says. "Not cheap. But we'll make it all back when we win Worlds."

Jacob holds out his palm. Han places the pill there.

"Now," Han says. It's not a suggestion.

Jacob tosses the pill back. The nanite burns all the way

down, settling like a hot stone in his stomach. For ten seconds, nothing changes. Then heat explodes outward from his core, racing through his veins, igniting nerve endings like fuses. His heart thunders against his ribs. His skin flushes red. Energy courses through him, unnatural and electric.

"Better," Han says, watching him closely. "Let's get back to training."

He signals to an assistant who wheels in a rack of bamboo sticks. Han selects one, testing its flexibility with a sharp bend.

"Form sequence six," Han orders. "Full speed. Continuous transitions."

Jacob moves into position. The new nanite makes his skin crawl with excess energy, like insects marching beneath the surface. He begins the sequence—punch, kick, teleport, strike, teleport, sweep, teleport.

The bamboo cracks against his shoulder when his elbow drifts too high. Again across his back when his transition comes a microsecond too slow. Each correction leaving a welt that will rise purple by morning. But Jacob doesn't question Han's methods. He still wants to win.

"Faster," Han demands.

Jacob pushes harder. Teleport, strike, teleport, kick. The world becomes a blur of transitions and impacts. His gi, already damp with sweat, now clings to him like a second skin, heavy and restricting. His ankle throbs with each land-ing, but the stamina nanite masks the worst of the pain.

Three senior students enter. Han gestures them forward.

"Rotation," he says. "Ninety-second intervals. Full contact."

The first student attacks. Jacob meets him with a combination of traditional strikes and teleportation, appearing behind, above, beside his opponent. The student is good, regional champion in his weight class, but he can't counter what he can't track. Jacob takes him down in forty-three seconds.

No rest. The second student jumps in immediately. Heavier, stronger, with a strength nanite that makes his punches like sledgehammers. Jacob evades rather than blocks, teleporting out of the impact zone, countering with strikes to vulnerable points. Sixty-five seconds, and the second student yields.

The third is more calculating. He's studied Jacob's patterns, anticipates the most likely teleport destinations. Jacob is forced to innovate, to teleport mid-strike, to materialize at unexpected angles. The combat stretches to eighty-four seconds before the third student finds himself in a submission hold he can't escape.

All three students rotate back in, fresh while Jacob continues. The stamina nanite keeps his muscles from failing, but his technique grows ragged at the edges. A teleport lands him two inches from where he intended. Another leaves him momentarily disoriented, the world tilting on its axis.

Han's bamboo stick lands across his knuckles when his guard drops. A painful strike behind his knee when his stance widens too much.

Two hours in, Han activates the new combat droids. Three mechanical opponents programmed with every fighting style in Han's database, their reaction times inhuman. They move like liquid shadows, attacking from multiple angles.

Jacob teleports into the air above them. The stamina nanite keeps his energy high, but something else is happening. He doesn't feel right. He's seeing two of everything. Feeling four. He lands, blocks a mechanical arm aimed at his ribs, counters with a kick that sends one droid skidding backward.

Ignoring the symptoms of fatigue, he teleports again, behind the second droid. As he materializes, the static in his vision intensifies, consuming his peripheral sight. He strikes blindly, feeling his fist connect with metal.

The third teleport breaks something inside him.

His vision bleeds to white. Complete whiteout, like staring into the sun. Jacob gasps, suspended in a moment of sensory overload. His knees buckle. The mat rushes up to meet him. The entire dojo disappears.

Voices reach him from a great distance. The combat droids power down with mechanical whines. Footsteps approach.

"Get up." Han's voice commands.

Jacob tries to respond, but his tongue feels too thick for his mouth. The white begins to recede, reality bleeding back in patches. He sees Han standing over him, expression cold as winter.

"I said, *get up*."

Jacob pushes himself to hands and knees. His arms shake with fine tremors he can't control. His gi is soaked through. Blood from his nose has spattered the mat beneath him.

"Can't train if you're on the floor," Han says. "Worlds won't be won from your knees."

Jacob finds his feet, swaying slightly. The whiteout has retreated, but left behind a hollow feeling, like someone scooped out parts of his consciousness and replaced them with nothingness.

His ankle throbs.

"Again," Han orders, stepping back.

Jacob steadies himself. The stamina nanite still burns in his system, pushing his exhausted body beyond natural limits. He focuses on a point across the dojo, preparing for another teleport.

For Worlds, he tells himself as the familiar compression begins. *For Mom. For the house. For everything we've fought for.*

The world tears apart, and Jacob with it.

When Han finally calls an end, Jacob's hands are trembling so badly he can barely untie his belt. His mother watches from across the room, her face tight.

"Meet me in my office," Han tells Jacob. "We need to discuss your Worlds preparation schedule."

Jacob nods. As Han disappears down the hallway, his mom meets him on the mats.

"You're not okay," she says quietly, reaching up to touch his face. Her palm is cool against his feverish skin.

"It's just training, Mom." He will not be responsible for putting her back in a shelter. They've put money away, but with Han taking seventy-five percent, it's not enough and it won't last forever. "Everyone gets tired."

She brushes his temple. "This isn't tired. This is something else." She glances toward the hallway where Han disappeared. "I'm talking to him."

"Mom, don't—"

But she's already moving. Jacob grabs his towel and follows on shaky legs.

He catches up to her outside Han's office. The door is closed, but his mom doesn't hesitate. She knocks sharply, three times.

"Master Han," she calls. "I need to speak with you."

The door opens. Han stands in the doorway. "Mrs. Shea. I was expecting your son."

"My son needs rest," she says, her voice firmer than Jacob has heard in years. "He's pushing too hard."

Han's eyes flick to Jacob, then back to his mom. "I just gave him a stamina nanite."

"Stamina burns out," she counters. "Look at him."

"I'm fine," Jacob insists, hiding his hands behind his back so they don't see them shaking. "The training is just more intense now. Worlds-level preparation."

Han nods. "Jacob understands what's required. What's at stake."

"What's at stake is his health," she says, her voice rising. "The headaches are getting worse. He barely sleeps. And the blackouts—"

"Blackouts?" Han's attention sharpens.

Jacob winces. He hasn't told Han about those. "It's nothing. Just zoning out sometimes."

"He stares at nothing," his mom continues, ignoring Jacob's attempt to minimize. "Minutes at a time. Sometimes longer. Yesterday morning I found him in the kitchen, standing over a broken glass. He didn't remember dropping it." Her voice cracks. "He didn't remember coming downstairs."

Han's expression doesn't change, but something shifts behind his eyes. "The nanites are working," he says. "Integration is deepening. It's expected."

"Expected?" She steps closer to Han. "My son is disappearing right in front of me, and you call it 'expected'?"

"Mom, please—"

"He's never been stronger," Han cuts in. "The teleportation sequences he executed today would have been impossible a month ago. His neural pathways are constantly adapting to his enhancement."

"He's not an *enhancement*," she says, her voice dropping dangerously low. "He's a seventeen-year-old boy. *My* boy."

Han's face hardens. "He's a champion. The face of modern fighting. The most marketable talent to emerge in a decade." He glances at Jacob again. "And he wants this. Don't you, Jacob?"

Jacob swallows. The throb behind his eyes intensifies, but he forces himself to nod. "I do. Worlds is everything we've worked for."

"Jacob, you don't have to—"

"The World Championship is in six weeks," Han says. "The training schedule is non-negotiable." His gaze returns to Jacob's mother, cold and final. "If Jacob wants to withdraw, that is his decision. But I think we all know what that would mean."

The threat hangs in the air. Withdraw, and everything

disappears—the house, the sponsorships, the financial security. Back to struggling. Back to invisibility.

"He won't withdraw," Han continues. "Because he understands sacrifice. The price of greatness." He steps back into his office. "Now if you'll excuse me, I have calls to make. Jacob, we'll review your schedule tomorrow."

The door closes with a decisive click, leaving Jacob and his mother alone in the hallway.

His mom stares at the closed door, tears welling in her eyes. "He doesn't see you," she whispers. "Only what you can do for him."

Jacob puts his arm around her shoulders. "It's just six more weeks," he says gently. "I'll win Worlds, and then we can renegotiate. Maybe even find a different manager." The words taste like ash in his mouth. He knows it won't be that simple. Nothing ever is with Han.

"Promise me, you'll tell me if it gets worse," his mother says, wiping away a tear. "No more hiding the blackouts. No more pretending."

Jacob agrees, though he's not sure he can keep that promise. Not when they're so close to everything he's fought for.

"Just six more weeks. I'll fight Worlds and then get out."

He doesn't tell her about the dreams—the ones where he teleports and never fully reappears. The ones where he scatters into blue light and stays that way, conscious but formless, watching the world from a place in between existence.

Six more weeks. He can hold himself together that long. He has to.

CHAPTER 14

FIFTY THOUSAND FACES blur into a wall of noise and expectation as Jacob steps onto the mat.

This is it. The moment every teleportation, every headache, every nosebleed has been building toward. World Championship.

"In the blue corner, undefeated National Champion, the Teleporting Terror—Jacob Shea!"

The crowd erupts. Jacob raises his fist, genuine excitement flowing through him. This is the moment when everything will change. All he has to do is win and he can take back the reins of his life.

His opponent waits in the opposite corner, still being announced. Takeshi Yamada. International champion. Six documented nanites in his system. A combat suite worth more than most people's homes.

Jacob bounces on his toes. His ankle throbs with a dull warning, taped tight but still weak from months of hard landings.

The referee calls them to center mat. Yamada's eyes meet his, dark and unreadable. They touch gloves.

"Clean fight. No strikes to the back of the head or spine. Signal if you need to tap out." The referee steps back. "Fight!"

Jacob doesn't wait. He activates the teleport, focusing on a point three feet to Yamada's left. The now-familiar void engulfs him for a heartbeat. Then he materializes exactly where he intended.

Yamada pivots, but too slowly. Jacob lands a clean hook to his temple. The impact travels up Jacob's arm, satisfying and solid. The crowd roars its approval.

Jacob teleports again, this time behind Yamada. Another strike, this one to the lower back. Yamada stumbles forward, clearly not expecting such aggression so early.

"Te-le-port! Te-le-port!" The chant builds from thousands of throats.

Jacob risks a glance ringside. Master Han stands among his betting partners, their wrist devices flashing with real-time odds and wagers. Han's face betrays nothing, but his posture radiates expectation. The bets placed on this fight could buy a small island. Maybe even a big one.

Yamada recovers, throwing a lightning-fast combination that forces Jacob to duck and weave. The Japanese fighter is good. Better than anyone Jacob has faced before. His strikes come from unexpected angles, testing Jacob's defenses.

Jacob teleports to the ceiling rafters. A gasp ripples through the crowd as heads tilt upward. He lets himself fall, concentrating on a point directly behind Yamada. Mid-descent, he teleports again. It's almost getting predictable, and yet Yamada staggers.

In the stands, Jacob spots his mother. Her hands grip the railing, knuckles white with tension. She didn't want to come, but he insisted. This is her moment as much as his.

"You got this, Jacob!" Someone screams from the crowd. His face flashes on the massive screens suspended above the ring. *The Teleporting Terror.* The face that launched a thousand enhancement sales.

Yamada circles, more cautious now. His guard is higher, his footwork more deliberate. Jacob presses forward with a combination—jab, cross, teleport, uppercut. The final blow connects with Yamada's jaw, snapping his head back.

The stamina nanite floods Jacob's system with artificial energy, masking the familiar fatigue that would normally follow multiple teleports. His body buzzes with power.

Two minutes into the first round, and Jacob is dominating. Yamada has landed only glancing blows, while Jacob's strikes have been clean and damaging. The crowd knows it. Han knows it. Jacob knows it.

Victory is within reach.

He teleports again, materializing above Yamada for a diving strike. As he descends, something catches his attention—a shift in Yamada's eyes. Not fear. Not confusion.

Calculation.

Jacob lands the strike, but something feels wrong. Yamada takes the hit too easily, rolling with it instead of trying to counter. He's waiting for something. But what?

No time to analyze. Jacob teleports to Yamada's right flank, preparing another combination.

That's when he sees it, the subtle weight shift in Yamada's

stance, the microscopic tell in his shoulder tension. He's anticipating Jacob's next move.

Too late to change course. Jacob is already teleporting, his body dissolving into blue energy as he targets a spot behind Yamada.

As Jacob rematerializes, Yamada is already moving—not where Jacob was, but where he will be. The champion pivots with inhuman speed, his leg sweeping low in a perfect arc that catches Jacob's bad ankle at the exact moment his molecules reform.

The impact comes with a sickening crack that echoes through the arena. Pain explodes up Jacob's leg, white-hot and blinding. His ankle gives way.

Jacob crashes to the mat, a heap of agony and disbelief. The world tilts sideways. The lights overhead blur and multiply. Fifty thousand faces contort in collective shock.

"Get up!" Han's voice cuts through the sudden hush. "Get up now!"

Jacob tries. His body responds by sending another wave of agony up his leg. The ankle won't bear weight. Won't even move without screaming protest.

Instinctively, he attempts to teleport away from the pain. But something is wrong. The teleport fails mid-process, leaving him frozen in a half-dissolved state for a terrifying second before his molecules snap painfully back into place.

The crowd's cheers transform into a cascade of boos and shouts.

"Stay down, son!" His mother's voice somehow reaches him. "Don't move!"

But Jacob can't stay down. Not here. Not now. Not with everything at stake.

He forces himself to his knees, pain shooting up his leg with every small movement. Yamada stands ready, waiting for Jacob to either continue or concede.

Jacob reaches for the teleport again. The nanite responds sluggishly, as if his pain is interfering with its function. The world begins to compress, then stops abruptly. His molecules protest, caught between states.

Another wave of boos crashes over the ring. Digital displays flash with updated betting odds, Han's partners frantically adjusting their positions as Jacob's chances plummet.

"Pathetic!" someone shouts from the crowd. "I want my money back!"

Jacob's touches his ankle. The joint moves in ways it shouldn't, bone grinding against bone beneath his fingers. Broken. Utterly shattered.

Yamada approaches cautiously, ready to continue. The referee steps between them, studying Jacob's condition.

"Can you continue?" the referee asks, his voice distant through the fog of pain.

Jacob opens his mouth to say yes.

But his body betrays him. The world spins violently, and he pitches forward onto the mat.

"The winner, by technical knockout, Takeshi Yamada!" The referee's words hammer into Jacob's skull, each syllable a fresh wound. Medics swarm the mat. Someone touches his ankle. Jacob screams. Twenty thousand spectators witness his humiliation in perfect high-definition, his failure projected onto screens the size of buildings.

"Don't move the joint." A medic's voice. "Compound fracture. We need to stabilize before transport."

Jacob's vision pulses in and out of focus. Sweat or tears blur his eyes. The arena lights drill into his retinas, too bright, too harsh. Faces in the crowd contort with disgust. The same people who chanted his name now jeer and shout obscenities.

"Waste of money!"

"Fraud!"

"Teleport home, loser!"

Jacob tries to sit up, but hands press him back to the mat. The medics attach a temporary brace to his shattered ankle. Pain radiates up his leg in nauseating waves. He catches glimpses of the giant screens above—his own face, pale and sweating, juxtaposed with replays of the decisive moment. His ankle breaking in slow motion. His body crumpling. His failure immortalized for the entertainment of thousands.

"Mom," he whispers, searching the blurred edges of the mat for her face.

In the stands, his mom pushes through rows of spectators. "That's my son! Let me through!"

Security forms a black-uniformed wall between her and the ring. "Medical personnel only," a guard states flatly. "Wait outside."

"But he needs me—"

"Ma'am, please step back."

His mother's face crumples as she's denied access. Beyond her, movement catches Jacob's eye. Han's betting partners are storming away from ringside, faces twisted with fury.

Han stands motionless among the exodus, his face carved

from stone. His eyes meet Jacob's across the distance. Jacob's stomach hollows.

"We need to get him to medical," a paramedic says, helping position a stretcher alongside Jacob.

"Wait." Jacob pushes away their hands. "I need to talk to my manager."

"Son, your ankle—"

"Just help me up." He grits his teeth against the pain. "Please."

Against their better judgment, two medics support Jacob as he rises to a standing position, his weight entirely on his good leg. The world tilts dangerously, but he forces himself to focus. He has to reach Han. Has to salvage something from this disaster.

Each hop toward ringside sends daggers of agony shooting through his body. The crowd's attention divides between Jacob's painful progress and Yamada's victory celebration at the opposite end of the arena. The champion raises his belt high, flashbulbs capturing his moment of triumph while Jacob limps toward what he hopes will be reassurance.

"Master Han," Jacob calls as he approaches. "I'm sorry. I don't know what happened. The teleport failed mid-jump and—"

"*What happened?*" Han hisses, stepping close enough that the nearby cameras can't capture his expression. "You failed. That's what happened."

Jacob flinches. "I'll train harder. Fix the integration issues. We can still—"

"There is no 'we' anymore." Han's voice rises, loud enough now for nearby cameras to pick up. Several turn in their direction. "You're finished. There is no way you can repay what I just lost."

The words don't register at first. They're too big. "But a regen nanite will fix it. I can be training again tomorrow. And next year—"

Han is shaking his head. "There won't be a next year for you. Everyone has seen you fail. Your opponents know you have a weakness."

"But the regen—"

"You will not be getting a regeneration nanite. I refuse to spend another cent on you."

"What are you saying?"

"I'm saying you're worthless to me now." Han's eyes are chips of black ice. "I invested everything in you. Three high class nanites. Years of training. Connections that can't be replaced." His hand cuts through the air in a dismissive gesture. "And you collapse when it matters most."

Jacob sways on his foot, the medics still supporting most of his weight. "I can fix this—"

"You owe too much. No one will sponsor you again. I'll be taking the house as collateral. And the car." Han straightens his tie.

Reality crashes down around Jacob. Everything they've built... all now tumbling into the abyss with his broken ankle.

"You can't do this," Jacob whispers. "We have nothing else."

"You should have thought of that before you failed." Han turns to a security guard. "Please escort Mr. Shea from the premises. He's no longer authorized personnel."

"Master Han, please—"

"Security!" Han's voice sharpens. "Now."

Two guards materialize beside Jacob, replacing the medics who step back with uncertain glances.

"Sir, he needs medical attention," one of the paramedics protests.

"There's a public hospital three blocks east," Han replies without looking at Jacob. "I suggest you take him there."

Jacob reaches for Han's arm, a final desperate attempt to change his mind. Han steps smoothly out of reach. "Don't make this more embarrassing than it already is," he says. "You're not the first fighter I've sponsored. You won't be the last."

The security guards take Jacob by the elbows, supporting his weight while simultaneously removing him from Han's presence. Jacob doesn't resist. Can't resist. His body has betrayed him as thoroughly as Han just has.

They guide him down a service corridor, away from the main exits where media and fans congregate. The roar of the crowd fades to a distant rumble behind concrete walls.

"Your mother can meet you at the south exit," one of the guards says, not unkindly. "We'll call her."

Jacob nods numbly.

The service exit opens onto a quiet side street. The guards help Jacob to a low concrete wall where he can sit without putting weight on his injury. "The ambulance will take about fifteen minutes in this traffic," the older guard says. "You gonna be okay till then?"

"Fine," Jacob manages. "Thanks."

They hesitate, then return inside, leaving Jacob. He leans

against the rough wall, the cool night air raising goosebumps on his sweat-dampened skin.

Jacob watches as Han emerges from another exit, surrounded by his remaining business associates. He slides into a waiting black car, door closing with a soft thud that somehow carries across the empty street.

Fuck You.

CHAPTER 15

THE DOCTOR DOESN'T LOOK at Jacob as he fits the temporary cast. Jacob can't decide whether it's because he's intimidated being around someone famous or disgusted with his latest performance. He shouldn't give a shit, but he finds himself waiting for the doctor to say something kind all the same.

"Your ankle is severely fractured in three places," the doctor says, finally looking up. "You'll need surgery to insert pins, followed by extensive physical therapy."

Jacob nods. Words feel useless.

"Unfortunately," the doctor continues, "your insurance verification has been declined. All procedures beyond emergency stabilization require payment arrangements."

His mother steps forward. "There must be some mistake. My son is—was—a sponsored athlete."

"*Was* being the operative word, ma'am." The doctor's face remains neutral. "Hospital policy is clear."

Three minutes later, security appears at the door—two men in intimidating uniforms with walkie-talkies clipped to their belts. One of them has kind eyes that don't match his job. The other stares at a point on the wall just above Jacob's head.

"We'll need you to vacate the treatment area," the kinder one says. "Once you've settled your account at the front desk, you're welcome to return."

His mother goes ramrod stiff. "My son can barely walk."

"We can provide a wheelchair to the exit," he offers. Then, lowering his voice, "I'm sorry."

Jacob slides from the table, his temporary cast clunking as he sets it on the ground. The pain medication they gave him when he arrived is wearing thin.

He reaches for his mother's shoulder. "Let's go."

The hallway stretches before them like a gauntlet. Fluorescent lights hum overhead, turning everyone the same sickly shade of almost-corpse. Jacob hobbles forward on a pair of crutches they've allowed him to take.

Other patients watch them pass. Security trails two paces behind. Jacob keeps his eyes on the floor. One crutch, then the other. The rhythmic tap of his good foot. The soft scrape of his cast. The endless linoleum squares becoming a hypnotic pattern he could drown in. Han could have given him a regen nanite. They're a fraction of the cost of teleportation. But no, even that mercy was too much for him.

At the front desk, a woman with artificially red hair doesn't look up from her screen. "That'll be sixteen thousand, eight hundred and forty-two dollars for services rendered."

His mom hands over her credit card.

The lady swipes it through the machine and an angry bleep is the only answer.

"Denied," the red head says.

Jacob frowns. "Try the other one."

His mom offers a second card. Same result. They stare at each other. Jacob has always known Han was ruthless, but this is a whole new low.

"Cash?" the red head asks.

"Do we look like we have that much cash on us?" Jacob snaps.

The red head flinches. "We don't take kindly to abusive customers."

Jacob almost explodes. Has the urge to ram her face into her keyboard. Instead, he grits his teeth and counts to ten.

"We don't have the money," his mom says.

They could make a run for it, but Jacob wouldn't get very far. Unless he teleported. But he's not going to leave his mom stranded.

"I see." The red head eyes them carefully. "The county clinic offers sliding scale services on Tuesdays and Thursdays. We'll be in touch about settlement."

With security still keeping a loose watch on them, they back away. The automatic doors slide open with a soft whoosh, expelling them into the night. Cold air slaps Jacob's face, a shock after the hospital's regulated warmth.

"There's an ATM across the street," his mom says, pointing to the glowing sign outside a convenience store. "Let's check our accounts."

Despite everything, there is a kernel of hope in Jacob's heart. After everything he gave to Han, he wouldn't take it all away from them, would he?

The walk across the street feels like miles. Each step

sends fresh spikes of pain shooting up his leg, but Jacob grits his teeth and keeps moving. One more step. Another.

The ATM's screen glows blue in the darkness. Jacob punches in his card number with shaking fingers. The machine whirs.

AVAILABLE BALANCE: $0.00

He stares at the number. Blinks. It doesn't change.

"Let me try mine," his mom says, reaching for her wallet.

AVAILABLE BALANCE: $0.00

Jacob's chest tightens. "Han," he whispers, the name like acid on his tongue.

One last chance. Jacob reaches for his back pocket, extracting a slim wallet. Inside is a card for an account he opened in secret six months ago, after Kenji warned him about Han's previous fighters. A safety net. Insurance against exactly this scenario. He didn't think he'd need it. But he guesses that was the ego talking.

He feeds the card into the machine, punches in the PIN.

AVAILABLE BALANCE: $0.00

"No." The word hisses out of his mouth. "No, no, no."

Jacob slams his fist against the ATM's metal frame. Once. Twice. Three times until his knuckles split and blood smears across the keypad. Something primal takes over, rage replacing thought. His foot lashes out, connecting with the base of the machine. His injured ankle screams in protest, the pain so intense his vision whites out for a second. He crumples, catching himself against the wall.

"Jacob!" His mother's hands are on his shoulders, steadying him.

"He took everything," Jacob gasps through the pain. "Every cent. Even the account he didn't know about."

"How could he—"

"I don't know how. But he did." Jacob slides down the wall until he's sitting on the cold concrete, his legs splayed before him. The money is gone. His career is gone. Everything they worked for, everything they sacrificed for—evaporated in a single night because his ankle couldn't hold together for one more round.

His mom kneels beside him, touches his shoulder.

"We'll figure something out," she says. "We always do."

Jacob looks up at her. Her eyes are red-rimmed but dry.

"I'm sorry," he whispers.

She shakes her head. "Not your fault. I knew Han was a dirty piece of shit. I let him use you. Because I saw your potential. And I wanted out of that shelter as much as you. This is on me."

"No," Jacob protests, giving her a feeble hug. "No, it's not. This is on Han."

His mom extends her hand. "Come on. Let's go home."

Jacob takes her hand. He rises unsteadily, using the crutches to balance. Together they wind their way to the bus station. The bus drops them a block from their home. Jacob's temporary cast catches on uneven sidewalk cracks, sending jolts of pain up his leg. But the pain in his ankle is nothing compared to what waits at the end of the street—strange cars parked in their driveway, lights blazing from windows that should be dark.

"Mom," he says, the word half whisper and half plea.

His mom's hand tightens on his arm. "I see them."

They approach their front door to find it standing open. Voices drift from inside, casual conversation punctuated by laughter. A man in an expensive suit exits carrying a box of Jacob's training gear, the SportFuel logo gleaming on the side.

"What do you think you're doing?" Jacob demands.

The man doesn't acknowledge them, walking past as if they're invisible.

Jacob steps over the threshold and freezes. Three of Han's sponsors direct movers who are methodically boxing up everything that isn't nailed down. The couch where Jacob and his mother watched movies is already gone, leaving rectangular indentations in the carpet. The kitchen table where they eat pancakes—also gone. The walls that once displayed his tournament certificates are bare, nail holes the only evidence they existed.

A woman in a charcoal blazer supervises as a mover wraps Jacob's national championship trophy in bubble wrap and nestles it in a box with his other awards. The golden figurine catches the light one last time before disappearing into darkness.

"That's mine," Jacob says. "I earned that."

The woman glances up, her face registering mild surprise. "Not according to the collateral terms of your management contract." Her gaze slides past him to another mover. "The second bedroom next. Everything goes."

Jacob turns toward the kitchen. A young man in a SportFuel polo shirt is emptying the cabinets, wrapping his mom's mismatched plates in newspaper. Then the cookie jar shaped like a fat cat that she bought at a yard sale. And the teapot she used for special occasions, though they never had special occasions.

In the corner, two technicians dismantle the digi-board where Jacob studied his opponents' moves, memorizing patterns and weaknesses. The screen that once displayed his heroes now goes dark as they disconnect cables and remove mounting brackets from the wall.

"You can't just—" Jacob starts, but stops when a tall man in an impeccably tailored suit descends the stairs, carrying a box of his mother's clothes.

It's Gregory Chen, one of Han's longest-standing sponsors. The man who clapped Jacob on the shoulder after nationals, who'd promised him "the world is yours now, kid." His eyes meet Jacob's without a flicker of recognition.

"Bathroom items are packed," Chen says to the woman in the blazer, looking through Jacob as if he doesn't exist.

Jacob takes a step forward, his injured ankle protesting. "This is our home."

Chen finally acknowledges him with a slight raise of one eyebrow. "*Was* your home. Master Han owns the deed."

His mom steps forward. "We haven't even had time to—"

"Time isn't really a luxury in these situations," Chen interrupts. "Master Han's investments require immediate recalibration when they... underperform." His eyes slide to Jacob's cast.

Another sponsor emerges from what was Jacob's bedroom. A smirk plays across his thin face when he spots Jacob.

"The teleporting wonder returns," the sponsor says.

Something hot and dangerous floods Jacob's veins. His

hands curl into fists. Three seconds pass while he catalogs the distance between himself and the man, calculates the force needed to drive his knuckles into that smirking mouth.

His mom's fingers close around his wrist. "Not now," she whispers. "Not like this."

Her words penetrate the red fog of his rage. He's outnumbered. Injured. And, worst of all, without legal ground to stand on. Those contracts he signed without reading—stacks of them, each one binding him tighter to Han with promises of glory and security. Security that vanished the moment his ankle shattered.

"Take what you can carry," Chen tells them. "The rest will be inventoried and liquidated against your outstanding debt."

Jacob's mom slips past him. Jacob follows, relying on the crutches. His room is barely recognizable. Drawers hang open, emptied. Closets stand bare. The bed where Jacob slept last night has been stripped to the mattress, which bears a bright yellow tag indicating its impending removal.

In the hallway, his mom opens the bottom drawer of a small chest. She extracts a framed photo.

"Just this," she whispers. "Just this one thing."

Jacob nods, throat tight. The photo contains everything that matters—his father, gone before Jacob could know him. The three of them in front of the restaurant before everything fell apart. Their entire history condensed to one framed photograph.

They leave without another word, walking away from everything they've built. Jacob doesn't look back. Can't bear to see the moving trucks being loaded with the evidence of his failure.

Jacob can't manage far with the crutches, so they find themselves at the nearest motel. It sits between a pawn shop and a liquor store, its neon VACANCY sign flickering. Jacob waits outside while his mom negotiates with the night clerk. The man finally nods, accepting cash—their last forty dollars, scrounged from her coat pocket.

Room 118 smells of cigarettes and something darker, more primal. Mildew creeps along the bathroom ceiling. The carpet squishes slightly underfoot. One small double bed occupies the center of the room, its brown bedspread thin from too many washings.

Jacob's mom sets the photo on the nightstand. She turns down the bedspread, checking for unwelcome surprises, then gestures for Jacob to sit.

"Let me help with your shoes."

Jacob sinks onto the mattress, which dips alarmingly in the middle. His mom kneels before him, gently easing off his right shoe. He only has one shoe. Where did the other one go? For some reason, this makes him laugh. Hysterically. For a good five minutes.

When he is calm again, they squeeze together on the narrow bed, Jacob's back against the wall, his mom on the outer edge. She strokes his hair, just as she did when he was small. When nightmares would wake him in the shelter, and her fingers would smooth away the fear.

"Sleep," she murmurs. "Tomorrow will be better."

Jacob stares at the water-stained ceiling, his body rigid with shame and helpless fury. He doesn't believe her. Can't.

Tomorrow won't be better. Neither will the day after. They've lost everything. Again.

Things aren't any better in the morning. And the pain in his ankle is worse. Jacob lies in the bed as him mom prepares to go to work, smoothing wrinkles from yesterday's blouse with damp palms.

"You should stay here," his mom says, pinning her hair back. "Rest your ankle. I'll talk to my supervisor, explain the situation."

Jacob shifts, wincing as the movement sends fresh daggers of pain up his leg. "What will you tell them?"

"The truth." She turns from the mirror and offers him a determined smile. "That my son is injured and we've had a setback."

A setback. Such a small, inadequate word for the collapse of their entire world.

"I'll be back at noon," she continues, collecting her purse. "We'll figure this out together."

Jacob nods, not trusting his voice. She bends to kiss his forehead, then straightens her shoulders and walks out, closing the door with a soft click.

The room feels emptier without her. Jacob stares at the water-stained ceiling, counting cracks to avoid counting problems. After twenty minutes of stillness, he forces himself upright. Sitting won't solve anything.

His contacts are still in his phone, for now, until the service gets cut off. There are people who owe him favors. People who profited from his rise. People who should help now.

He pulls up his contacts, starting with the biggest sponsor. SportFuel. The company that plastered his face across the city on digi-displays. The company that promised him "a long and mutually beneficial relationship."

The receptionist's voice is crisp, professional. "SportFuel, how may I direct your call?"

"Jacob Shea for Marcus Reid."

"One moment please."

Three minutes of hold music, then: "Mr. Reid's office."

"This is Jacob Shea. I need to speak with Marcus about my contract situation."

A pause. "I'm sorry, Mr. Reid is unavailable. Would you like his voicemail?"

Jacob recognizes the brush-off. "When will he be available?"

"I can't say. His schedule is quite full."

"Please tell him it's urgent. About my endorsement contract."

Another pause, longer this time. "Mr. Reid asked not to be disturbed with calls regarding your contract. It's been terminated as per section 8, paragraph 3—failure to maintain competitive status."

The call disconnects before Jacob can respond. He stares at the phone, a hollow feeling expanding in his chest.

He tries NanoBoost next. Then PerformanceEdge. Then the three smaller supplement companies that paid him for social media posts. Each call follows the same pattern:

"Can't help you, Mr. Shea."

"We've moved in another direction."

"The contract specifically states—"

"I'll pass your message along, but don't expect—"

By the tenth call, a pattern emerges in the rejections. They all know. They all mention "recent developments" or "your current situation." Some sound genuinely regretful. Most don't bother pretending.

The final number in his contacts belongs to BioTech Nutrition, a company that approached him after nationals.

"BioTech, this is Alicia."

"Jacob Shea calling for Tom Werner."

"Oh." The single syllable carries volumes. "Mr. Werner is expecting your call, actually. One moment."

Jacob straightens, wincing as his ankle shifts against the chair leg. Someone expecting his call. Someone who might help.

"Jacob." Werner's voice is carefully neutral. "I was wondering when you'd reach out."

"Tom, I need—"

"I'm afraid we can't help you." The words come quick. "Master Han advised us of your... situation. The contractual violations. The outstanding debts."

Jacob's grip tightens on the phone. "What did he tell you?"

"Enough. The teleportation nanite alone cost more than my annual salary. Not to mention the training facilities, the medical support, the promotional investments." Werner sighs. "Han's been clear. Anyone who assists you will be blacklisted from his network. And his network is... extensive."

The ember of hope extinguishes. "I see."

"For what it's worth, I'm sorry. You had potential."

Had. Past tense. Like his career. Like his future.

Jacob is still staring at his phone when his mom returns.

It's not anywhere near noon. Her face tells him everything before she speaks.

"I no longer have a job," she says simply, sinking into the chair beside him. "Apparently the parent company has connections to SportFuel. They were 'regretfully forced to terminate my position due to restructuring.'"

Jacob closes his eyes. Han's reach extends further than he imagined, a poison spreading through every aspect of their lives.

"And you?" she asks.

"Nobody will touch me. Han's made sure of it."

A beat of silence passes. So loud it screams in Jacob's ears.

"We can't afford another night at the motel," his mom says.

Jacob nods. They both know what comes next.

By sunset, they're back at the old shelter. But he's seventeen now. They can't take him at the women and children's shelter. An hour later, they find themselves setting up cardboard beneath a concrete overpass, joining the invisible community of those who've slipped through society's cracks. The space smells of urine and desperation. Three other makeshift shelters line the wall.

An older man with a weathered face approaches, offering a flattened box. "For your leg," he says, nodding at Jacob's cast. "Keeps the damp off."

Jacob accepts with murmured thanks. The man shuffles back to his own corner without another word.

His mom arranges their meager belongings—the photo, her purse, Jacob's phone with its rapidly dying battery. Then she creates a semblance of shelter from discarded cardboard and a plastic tarp someone abandoned.

"It's just temporary," she says.

Jacob sits with his back against concrete, ankle throbbing, watching people walk past on the street above without seeing them. Men in business suits. Women in comfortable shoes hurrying home. Couples laughing together. He could teleport somewhere else. But what good would it do?

"I'm sorry," he whispers to his mother.

She takes his hand. "We're together. That's all that matters."

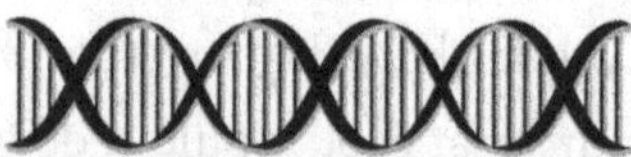

Jacob makes a quarter disappear between his fingers and reappear behind a little girl's ear. Basic sleight of hand, not teleportation. He's saving the real magic for the finale.

The shelter's common room isn't his favorite place, but the children's laughter cuts through the heaviness like sunlight through smog.

"Again!" the girl demands, her eyes wide with wonder. Seven years old, maybe eight. Reality yet to slap her in the face.

"One more trick," Jacob says.

The crowd of children expands as word spreads. Five kids become eight, then twelve. Jacob rolls his shoulders, loosening the tightness there. Time for the main event.

"Watch closely," he tells them, holding up his empty hands.

Jacob focuses on a point three feet to his right. The familiar compression begins, the strange suspension between atoms, then the snap back to reality as he disappears and reappears instantly.

The children gasp. Their small hands reach out to touch the space where he stood a second before.

"How'd you do that?" a boy with a shaved head asks, poking the air as if searching for wires or mirrors.

Jacob shrugs. "Nanites. Like superpower pills."

He doesn't mention the nosebleeds that still come sometimes. Or the headaches that drill into his skull after too many teleports. Or the mornings when he wakes up in strange corners of the shelter, having teleported in his sleep again. At least his ankle is better. Six weeks will heal most broken bones. But not his rage. That's a simmering pot of lava in danger of boiling over any minute of any day.

"Can you go anywhere?" another child asks.

"Only short distances."

He performs three more jumps, each one simpler than anything he would have attempted in competition. Blink from one side of the circle to the other. Vanish from in front of one child to appear before another. The audience's excitement builds with each demonstration, their small faces alight.

From across the room, Jacob catches his mother's eye. She sits at one of the scarred folding tables, mending a tear in what looks like someone else's shirt. Work for extra privileges, probably. Better shower times or an extra food voucher. She smiles when she sees him looking, her face brightening in the way that squeezes Jacob's heart. Like he's still her champion. Like they aren't living in a concrete box with sixty strangers. At least they're not on the streets. It took a week, but they finally found a shelter that would take them both.

"Do the ceiling one!" calls a gap-toothed boy who's seen Jacob's routine before.

"Fine," Jacob says. "Last one for today."

He targets a spot near the fluorescent lights, eight feet up. The displacement is rougher this time, his body protesting the vertical shift. He appears briefly near the ceiling, hovers for half a second, then drops down, landing in a crouch that sends a twinge through his healed ankle.

The children erupt in cheers and applause. Jacob bows theatrically.

"Alright, show's over," he tells them. "Go bother someone else now."

They disperse reluctantly, already discussing what they witnessed, embellishing details in the way children do.

The shelter houses twice as many people as it was designed for. Bunk beds line the walls of the main sleeping area like filing cabinets for human beings. Privacy is a memory. Clean air is a dream. But at least they're not under the overpass anymore.

Jacob makes his way toward his mother, navigating around residents clustered in little islands of conversation. The woman with the turtle shell nanite sits hunched over a book, her spine fused into a permanent stoop. The lights overhead flicker as he passes the man whose left arm phases in and out of visibility—a stealth nanite gone wrong, maybe, or a camouflage enhancement that couldn't fully integrate.

"You're getting better at the landing," his mother says as he reaches her. She holds up the shirt she's mending. "Almost finished with this one."

"They treating you okay?" Jacob asks, keeping his voice

low. He hates that she takes on extra work. Hates even more that he can't find a job to support them both.

"Of course. The coordinator even mentioned there might be a spot opening in the kitchen next week."

Jacob nods, swallowing the acid that rises in his throat. His mother worked as an executive assistant before everything fell apart.

"Hey, Shea!" someone calls from across the room. "Get over here!"

Jacob turns to see a group of people gathering around the ancient television bolted to the wall in the corner. The volume is cranked up.

"What's going on?" he asks, helping his mother to her feet.

"National broadcast. President Bear."

The name is enough to make them hurry over. The crowd parts to give them a view of the screen. President Bear's face fills the display, his features sharp beneath carefully styled hair. Red irises, the result of his own enhancement, stare out from the screen.

"This is a national announcement," Bear begins, his deep voice commanding attention. "All unadjusteds age twelve and over will now be required to take a nanite to enhance their abilities."

The room goes silent. Even the children stop playing.

"With threats and competition from overseas, we must do more to further the strength of our country," President Bear continues. "The program begins immediately. Mobile enhancement units will be dispatched to all major cities, beginning with schools, community centers, shelters, and public housing. Your cooperation is not optional, but your service to a stronger nation will be rewarded."

Jacob snorts, the bitter irony hitting him all at once. The universe's cosmic joke. He's already more enhanced than most people in the city. Several nanites deep, including a Class 10 teleportation. And where did it get him? A bunk in a shelter and a mother who mends other people's clothes.

"Those who resist will face unfortunate circumstances," Bear warns, his red eyes seeming to stare directly at Jacob. "This is not a request, but a requirement for continued citizenship."

A tremor runs through the crowd. Someone curses. A child starts crying.

Jacob turns to his mother, ready to share the dark humor of their situation—how he's already answered the president's call and ended up here anyway. The joke dies in his throat when he sees her face.

She's gone pale, one hand pressed to her mouth. Her eyes meet his, wide with a fear he hasn't seen since the night they lost their home.

"Mom?" he whispers.

And that's when he gets it. The reality crashes down. His mother is unadjusted. So are most of the people in this shelter. They're exactly who Bear is targeting. They're the ones who will be forced to take whatever nanites the government decides are necessary.

Jacob's mind races with images of his own enhancements —the headaches, the nosebleeds, the uncontrolled teleporting. The woman with the turtle shell. The man whose arm flickers in and out of existence. Failed integrations. Bodies rebelling against foreign code.

"They can't make us," someone says from the back of the crowd. "They can't force us to change our DNA."

But the fear in the room says otherwise. They all know what President Bear is capable of. What his administration has already done to those who resist.

Jacob mutters an excuse about the bathroom and walks away before anyone can see the panic in his eyes. His mind races through options, each one worse than the last. Run? To where? Fight? Against what? An entire government enforcement system? The bathroom door creaks as he pushes it open. He needs a plan. Now.

Jacob splashes cold water on his face, watching it drip from his chin into the rust-stained sink. His reflection stares back at him from the scratched mirror—hollow-cheeked, dark circles under his reptilian eyes.

A small window sits high on the wall, maybe eight inches tall by fifteen wide. Too small for an adult to crawl through, but big enough to... what? Signal someone? Who would come for them?

Jacob's hand trembles as he reaches for a paper towel. He could teleport his mother out of here. But teleporting with a passenger drains him twice as fast, and he's already operating at half capacity. He might manage one jump, maybe two. Not enough to get them safely away.

Maybe he should find Kenji. His old training partner would help, if Jacob could find him. If he wasn't competing somewhere with Han's support. If, if, if.

A stark sound invades his thoughts. Boots on linoleum.

Heavy, authoritative footsteps. Multiple sets. The main entrance.

They're already here.

Jacob abandons the paper towel and moves to the bathroom door. He presses his ear against it. More footsteps. Orders being barked in clipped tones. Someone crying.

He pulls the door open a crack and peers through.

The shelter's main area has transformed in the minutes since he left. Men and women in crisp uniforms with red armbands. Nanite enforcement reps. They set up portable stations near the entrance. They're checking IDs against tablets, separating residents into groups.

Bulks flank the exits. They're enormous soldiers with armored skin. Fire-retardant, bulletproof, nearly indestructible except for those four weak points. Back of both knees. Throat. Base of the skull. Jacob recalls the information from opponents he faced on the mat.

"Form a line according to your designated numbers," a rep announces through a portable amplifier. "Unadjusteds will proceed to the buses for transport to processing centers."

Jacob scans the space for his mother. He spots her across the room, being herded toward the front doors with a group of older residents.

There is no time for a plan.

Jacob focuses on a spot directly behind the bulk guarding his mother's group. The compression begins, familiar but more painful than usual—the result of too many jumps today.

He materializes precisely where he aimed. Without hesitation, Jacob drives his heel into the back of the soldier's knee

—the vulnerability point where the armor doesn't fully cover the joint.

The bulk crashes down with a startled grunt. Jacob grabs his mother's hand.

"Jacob!" she gasps.

"We need to go. Now."

Shouts erupt as the other bulks notice their fallen comrade. An enforcement rep reaches for something at her belt—a weapon, a radio... Jacob doesn't wait to find out. He focuses on a spot near the emergency exit, pulling his mother close.

"Hold on."

The compression comes harder this time, stretching him thin, his molecules protesting the extra weight of another person. They materialize across the room, his mother staggering as her feet find the floor.

The room erupts. Residents scream, some attempting to rush the exits, others cowering against walls. Enforcement reps draw stun batons, their tips crackling with blue electricity. The bulks converge, moving with surprising speed for their size.

"Keep moving," Jacob tells his mother, pushing her toward the exit. "I'll hold them off."

A bulk charges them. Jacob teleports directly into its path, materializing just long enough to strike at its throat before blinking away again. The bulk clutches at its neck, momentarily incapacitated.

Jacob reappears beside his mother, only to find two reps blocking their path. He doesn't hesitate. Teleport. Strike.

Teleport. Strike. His body becomes a weapon, appearing and disappearing faster than the eye can track.

For a moment, he's the champion again. The unstoppable *Teleporting Terror*.

But the shelter is filling with more enforcement personnel. They pour through the main entrance, cutting off escape routes. A bulk swings at Jacob, missing by inches as he teleports away.

"Jacob!" His mother's scream.

He's lost track of her. Jacob teleports to the ceiling rafters, clinging to a support beam as he scans the crowd below. There. Being dragged toward the buses by two enforcement reps. Her eyes are wild, searching for him.

Jacob doesn't think. He teleports directly into the group, taking out the first rep with a spinning kick that connects with the man's temple. The second rep releases his mother to draw her weapon, but Jacob is already teleporting again, appearing behind her with a strike to the kidney.

"Run!" he shouts to his mother.

She turns toward him, reaching—

The impact catches Jacob mid-teleport. A bulk's massive fist connects with his side as he materializes, sending him crashing into the wall. The pain is blinding, immediate. His concentration shatters, the teleportation cutting off halfway.

Jacob struggles to his feet, vision swimming. Three bulks form a semicircle around him, barricading him from his mother. She's being forced toward the bus doors now, too far to reach with a conventional attack.

He needs one more teleport. Just one more.

Jacob focuses, drawing on reserves he's not sure are there.

The compression begins, his molecules separating as he targets a spot near the bus. The world stretches, then snaps. But he materializes three feet short of his goal, his depleted energy failing him. A stun baton catches him in the ribs before he can recover.

Electricity courses through him. His muscles lock, sending him crashing to the ground. The concrete is cold against his cheek. With double vision, he sees his mother at the bus door, her face turned toward him one last time.

Their eyes meet across the distance, a moment suspended in time, full of everything they can't say. Her lips form his name. Then hands push her forward, and she disappears into the bus.

Jacob tries to stand. His body won't respond. The electricity still flows through his nerves, rendering him helpless. He can only watch as the bus door hisses closed. The engine rumbles to life. Tires turn.

And his mother is gone.

CHAPTER 17

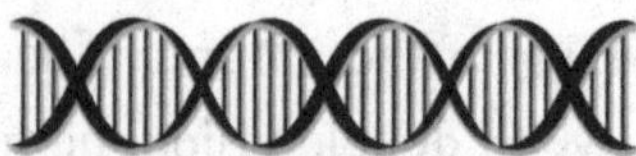

Jacob searches the city for seven days. There are soldiers everywhere and he maxes out his teleporting skills avoiding them. One time he wakes up in a dumpster after he blacks out. Couldn't remember if he'd crawled in there himself or someone put him there.

An entire week and he still has no idea where his mother is. Jacob stands outside a processing center. It's a gray monolith surrounded by bulks and enforcement agents. Could his mother be in there? He can't remember how many he's checked.

He approaches the checkpoint. The line crawls forward, each person scanned and questioned before being allowed to submit an inquiry. Jacob's stomach growls. He can't remember when he last ate.

"Next," barks the enforcement agent, not looking up from her tablet.

Jacob steps forward. "I'm looking for my mother. Elizabeth Shea. She was taken from the Riverside Shelter last week."

The agent's eyes flick up, lingering on his face. Recognition sparks and dies. "ID."

He has nothing to show. His ID, like everything else, was left behind when the shelter was raided. "I don't have one."

"No ID, no information." She waves him away, already looking past him to the next person in line.

"Please." Jacob plants his hands on the counter. "She's all I have."

The agent's expression hardens. "Step back now, or I'll have you removed."

Two bulks shift their weight, ready to intervene. Jacob backs away. Can't risk another confrontation. Not when he's still bruised from the last one.

He walks twenty blocks to the next processing center, narrowly avoiding several fights breaking out on the streets. He has the urge to join in. Weird. The last seven days his dreams have been filled with rage and violence. And it's getting worse. He has to keep checking himself.

The second processing center yields the same result. So does the third. By sunset, Jacob slumps against the wall of an alley, exhaustion dragging at his bones. He closes his eyes, just for a moment.

"—shipping them out to the compounds outside the city," a voice says, startling him awake.

Two sanitation workers stand at the alley entrance, sharing a cigarette. Jacob stays perfectly still, listening.

"My cousin works transport. Says they've moved thousands already."

"What for? Labor?"

A shrug. "Government doesn't share details. Just that they go in, nothing comes out."

The conversation drifts to sports, then weather. Jacob waits until they move on before pushing himself up. Compounds. Outside the city. That's where he needs to look.

Morning finds him at the transportation hub, watching government vehicles come and go. Buses with blacked-out windows. Unmarked vans. Heavy security at every entrance. No way in without credentials.

"Jacob Shea?"

Jacob turns, muscles tensing. A man in a tailored suit approaches, eyebrows raised in surprise.

"It *is* you. Didn't expect to see the Teleporting Terror slumming it at a bus station."

The name stings. Jacob doesn't recognize the man. Maybe an old fan.

"Thought you'd be living the high life," the man says.

"I'm looking for information," Jacob says. "About the unadjusted compounds."

The man blinks. "You and me both."

"My mother was taken. I need to find her."

"My wife." The man nods. "Unadjusted. They're being held in government facilities outside major cities. No visitors. No communication. They're being... processed."

The way he says the word makes Jacob's skin crawl. "Processed how?"

"Enhanced, I imagine. President Bear was quite clear about his vision for a fully adjusted society. But no one can get anywhere near those compounds. Security is... extensive."

"I need to try."

"You need to be realistic." The man adjusts his cuffs. "Your mother. My wife. They're government property now. And in case you haven't noticed, alts are killing people in the streets."

He hasn't. Not really. Just teleports away when he sees a hint of trouble. Nothing to do with him.

"Good luck," the man says.

"You too," Jacob says, turning away.

"If you're truly desperate," the man calls after him, "there's a reward for information leading to Silver Melody's capture. President Bear's offering a fortune. Enough to buy a new life."

Jacob pauses, the words piercing through his exhaustion. A fortune. Enough to bribe officials. Enough to find his mother.

"Silver Melody is Dr Melody's daughter," the man continues. "They're both on the run. Apparently there's a cure..." the man gestures toward Jacob's obvious enhancements. "For alterations."

A cure? No more headaches? Nose bleeds? Blacking out? Waking up in the middle of nowhere? And he can't deny the forked tongue was a mistake. Makes eating and drinking twice as hard. He'd pay a hefty sum for a cure.

The idea follows him through the day, lurking in the corners of his mind. Find Silver Melody. Turn her in. Use the money to save his mother.

It would be simple. He has the skills. The teleportation. The combat training. He could do what an army of bulks has failed to accomplish.

As night falls, Jacob finds shelter in an abandoned building, curling up in a corner that offers some protection from the wind that whistles through broken windows. His stomach cramps with hunger.

Silver Melody.

The name surfaces again. The solution to his problems. The key to finding his mother.

And yet.

Jacob stares at his hands in the dim light. Turning in Silver would mean becoming exactly what Han trained him to be. A weapon. A tool for someone else's agenda. It would mean betraying someone fighting against the system that took his mother.

"I won't do it," he whispers to the empty room. "I won't be that person."

No. He won't be the one to betray Silver Melody. Won't trade one person's freedom for another's. There has to be another way to find his mother.

The next day, after he is almost arrested, and then killed in a fight between highly enhanced and out of control alts, Jacob leaves the city. There is no point in him being there anymore. He finds shelter in a warehouse. It smells of damp and forgotten things. Judging by the thick layer of dust on the ground, no one has been here in weeks.

Jacob sleeps in the back office for three nights without disturbance. The office offers a decent vantage point. Clear sight lines to all entrances. It has a broken window and a worn couch that smells of mildew but it beats sleeping on concrete. Best of all, there are cases of protein bars and bottled water stacked in a corner. More food than he's seen since his mother was taken.

Jacob tears open another protein bar, forcing himself to

eat slowly. His stomach has shrunk these past weeks. Too much at once makes him sick.

His head snaps up when he hears voices. Distant but getting closer.

He freezes mid-bite, listening.

Jacob slides from the couch to the floor, creeping toward the office window that overlooks the main warehouse floor. He peers over the sill.

Several figures move through the shadows below, dressed in what looks like army fatigues. Green and brown camouflage. Military boots. One is massive, easily seven feet tall with shoulders like granite blocks. Another is leaner, quick movements, male. A third is female, smaller but moving with unmistakable authority.

Enforcers. Have to be. Coming to sweep the warehouse, round up anyone hiding from the enhancement program.

Jacob pulls back from the window. He has three options: run, hide, fight. Running means revealing himself. Hiding means discovery when they search thoroughly. Fighting...

Fighting is the only advantage he has.

He takes a deep breath, centers himself. One surprise attack could give him the edge he needs.

Footsteps on the metal stairs. Coming up to the office level. Jacob positions himself behind the door, calculates distances and angles.

The door creaks open. The massive one enters first, ducking his head to clear the frame. Jacob focuses on a point directly behind him, feeling the familiar compression begin.

The world stretches, snaps. He's behind the giant now, launches a precision strike at the base of the neck.

But the bulk spins faster than seems possible, arm blocking Jacob's attack. Not the anticipated response. Jacob teleports again, this time materializing on the other side of the room near the female figure.

She turns, her face coming into focus for a split second—intense silver eyes, dark hair. Something familiar about her that Jacob can't process because he's already launching another strike. His fist connects with her shoulder, but instead of staggering back, she absorbs the impact.

What the hell?

Jacob teleports again, aiming for the third figure who's moving to flank him. Strike to the solar plexus. Teleport. Kick to the knee. Teleport. Uppercut.

The fight erupts in a blur of movement. Jacob becomes a phantom, appearing and disappearing across the room. His training takes over.

But these aren't ordinary enforcers. The female recovers instantly from each blow, as if drawing strength from the impacts. The bulk moves with shocking speed for his size. The third man anticipates Jacob's patterns, positioning himself to intercept.

"Stop!" the female shouts. "We're not—"

Jacob doesn't let her finish. Can't risk hesitation. He teleports again, this time aiming for the ceiling beam to gain height advantage.

The compression begins, but something's wrong. The transition stretches too long, his molecules reluctant to reassemble. Fatigue. Overextension. The price of too many jumps on too little food.

He materializes off-target, listing to one side. His vision

tunnels, black edges creeping in. The momentary disorientation is all they need.

The female moves with startling quickness, closing distance while he's vulnerable. She strikes his chest. The impact resonates through him, sapping strength from his limbs.

Jacob staggers backward, trying to teleport again. Nothing happens.

The bulk and the third man converge from opposite sides. Jacob manages a defensive stance, blocking the first grab attempt, but his movements are sluggish. The bulk catches his arm, twists it behind his back with inexorable strength. The other man secures his second arm, efficiently pinning him.

"Easy now," the bulk rumbles, his grip firm but not crushing. "We're not looking to hurt you."

Jacob struggles against their hold, finding no weakness. "You're army," he spits. "Enforcement. Coming for anyone who's hiding."

The female approaches cautiously, silver eyes studying him. "We're not enforcement."

Jacob gestures with his chin toward their clothing. "The fatigues. Military issue."

Jacob reassesses. The bulk is not like the ones working for enforcement. This one's eyes hold intelligence, restraint.

The bulk looks down at his camouflage pants and chuckles. "Easy mistake to make. But no. We're not army."

Jacob's shoulders slump as the fight drains out of him. Exhaustion crashes in waves. His head pounds from teleportation overuse. Days of running, hiding, searching—all catching up.

"Then who?" he asks.

The pressure on Jacob's arms eases slightly, but the bulk and the other man maintain their grip. The female studies him like he's a wild animal that might still have fight left.

"Who are you?" she asks.

Jacob stares back, recognition hitting like a thunderbolt. The face from wanted posters. From emergency broadcasts. From whispered conversations in back alleys and shelters.

"You're Silver Melody," he breathes, the words escaping before he can think better of it.

Her expression sharpens. She takes a half-step back, exchanging glances with her companions. "How do you know who I am?"

Jacob presses himself against the wall, feeling the cool concrete through his thin shirt. His eyes dart between the group. There are more of them. More than he can count. All of them look enhanced.

"Everyone knows who you are," he says. "The reward—"

The bulk moves with shocking speed. One moment he's holding Jacob's arm, the next his forearm presses against Jacob's windpipe, cutting off his words.

"Are we going to be able to let you leave this warehouse?" the bulk asks, voice deceptively soft for someone so massive.

Jacob's arms twist reflexively against the hold. His skin ripples, digi-tattoos swirling across his exposed forearms in response to his stress. The characters form, dissolve, and reform.

"Not going to turn you in," Jacob chokes out, desperate for air.

The bulk doesn't release him.

Silver takes another step forward, her eyes never leaving Jacob's face. "How do I know I can trust you?"

The pressure on Jacob's throat eases enough for him to speak. He coughs, drawing in a painful breath. "Because there's no place for me out there anymore. I've been hiding for days."

Something shifts in Silver's expression. Sympathy?

Movement from the doorway catches Jacob's eye. Another guy enters—lean, intelligent face, sandy brown hair. He carries a bottle of water, approaches cautiously.

"Out with it then," the newcomer says. "Who are you and where did you come from?"

He offers the water, which Jacob takes with shaking hands after the bulk releases his throat. The cool liquid soothes his parched throat, and he drinks greedily before answering.

But before he can speak, Silver interrupts. "You're Jacob Shea."

"Jacob *who*?" A female with purple butterfly wings flutters into Jacob's peripheral vision.

Jacob lowers the bottle, wiping his mouth with the back of his hand. He nods once, a single confirmation.

Another younger male pumps a fist into the air. "Hell yes, you are! Dude, I knew I recognized you. What happened? You got wiped out of the World Championships. Had your legs swept out before you could teleport..."

"Thanks for the reminder," Jacob says bitterly.

The guy's enthusiasm falters, realization dawning. "Shit. Sorry. That was... that was really tactless." He rubs the back of his neck, embarrassment flushing his cheeks. "I just... I followed your whole career, man. Every match. That spinning teleport knockout against Vega? Some hardcore action right there." He holds out a hand for a knuckle punch.

After a couple of seconds, Jacob obliges. "Thanks for the support."

"So what happened?" Silver asks. "You dropped out of the circuit after that competition?"

"My dojo master disowned me," Jacob replies. "When he lost money on a bet, took my house to pay for my debts. We left, then Mom and I got separated when all the shit hit the fan."

"Where's your mom now?" the sandy-haired guy asks.

"I don't know," Jacob replies.

"Unadjusted or..."

"Unadjusted," Jacob says.

The bulk takes a step back, giving Jacob more space. "I'm Joe," he says, the introduction unexpected. "Joe Rucker."

"Matt Lawson," the sandy-haired guy adds.

Silver doesn't offer her name. Doesn't need to. "Why were you looking for information about the reward on me?"

Jacob flinches. Of course she caught that. "I wasn't. Not actively. But people talk. Officials talk. Someone recognized me at a transport center, mentioned the bounty. Said I could buy a new life if I helped find you."

"And did you consider it?" Silver asks bluntly.

The question hangs in the air. Jacob looks away, shame burning in his gut. "For about five minutes. I was desperate."

"But you didn't," Matt says.

"No." Jacob meets Silver's gaze directly. "I'm done being someone's weapon. Done fighting for the wrong side."

Silver studies him for a long, uncomfortable moment. Jacob forces himself not to look away. His reptilian eyes make people uneasy. Make them see him as something other than human. But Silver doesn't flinch.

"Your mother," she says finally. "You mentioned you got separated?"

"They took her. A couple weeks ago. Enforcement agents raided the shelter. I fought—" Jacob swallows. "I fought, but there were too many. They loaded all the unadjusteds onto buses. No one will tell me where."

Understanding passes between the resistance members. Something unspoken but clear.

"The compounds," Joe says quietly. "That's where they're taking all unadjusteds now."

"I've tried to find them," Jacob says, frustration bleeding into his voice. "Been searching ever since they took her. No one will tell me anything."

Matt exchanges looks with Silver, silent communication passing between them. "We know where they are," he says carefully. "We've been mapping them. Planning."

Hope flares in Jacob's chest. "You know where my mother might be?"

"We can't promise that," Silver cautions. "But we know where to look."

Jacob straightens, finding new strength. "Then I need to go there. I need to find her."

"It's not that simple," Matt says. "The compounds are

heavily guarded. Multiple layers of security. Bulk patrols. Hellhounds."

"I don't care," Jacob insists. "I'll figure it out."

Silver steps forward. "Alone, you'd never make it past the outer perimeter. But we're not going in alone."

Jacob stills, understanding dawning. "You're planning something."

"Not planning anymore," Joe says. "Doing."

Silver nods once, decisive. "We're going to break them all out. Every unadjusted in every compound."

The magnitude of it staggers Jacob. Not just a rescue, but a revolution.

"Are you in?" Silver asks, direct and unflinching.

"Absolutely." The word leaves Jacob's mouth without hesitation. Finding his mother, freeing her from whatever nightmare Bear has created... it's the only thing that matters.

"Well, that was easy," says a female voice from the shadows.

Jacob turns, startled by the new arrival. A young woman hovers—literally hovers—above the stacked boxes, suspended by vibrant green wings. Her dark hair falls in perfect waves around shoulders.

She floats closer, wings creating small currents that stir the dust motes in the slanted afternoon light. Her eyes narrow as she examines Jacob's face. "So how far can you teleport?"

Jacob hesitates. Pride wants him to claim the range and endurance of his competition days. Reality is less impressive. "Short distances only. Few hundred feet max. And maybe... eight jumps before I need recovery. Used to be more, but—"

"But you haven't been eating right," Joe finishes for him, understanding in his deep voice. "Nanites need fuel. Especially Class Tens."

"We have food," Silver says. "Supplies. We can get you back to strength."

The younger guy grins. "Man, having a teleporter on the team? That changes everything. We could get past the outer barriers without tripping alarms."

"If he's trustworthy," Matt says.

"I trust him," Silver says, surprising everyone, Jacob included. "He had every reason to try for the bounty on my head. He didn't."

The group begins discussing logistics—safe houses, supply routes, security. Jacob listens, absorbing the information while cataloging each member. Silver with her natural authority and silver eyes. Matt with his strategic mind. Joe the bulk with unexpected gentleness. Kyle with his enthusiastic energy. Erica with her butterfly wings and sharp edges.

But Jacob can't keep his eyes off the girl with green wings with feathers that catch the light in emerald and jade shimmers.

She feels his gaze, looks up. Their eyes meet across the dusty warehouse office. Hers are a deep, emerald green that match her wings.

Jacob looks away first, unsettled by the intensity of her attention. By the strange flutter in his chest that has nothing to do with teleportation or hunger or the mission ahead.

For the first time since his world collapsed, Jacob feels something beyond anger and desperation. Something small and unexpected.

Curiosity.

The End

If you enjoyed Jacob's story, I'd be ever so grateful for a review. You can leave one here:

https://geni.us/JacobShea

If you want to know what happens to Jacob now, check out *The Unadjusteds*:

https://geni.us/Theunadjusteds

Read on for the first chapter of the next origin story, **Sawyer Watson**.

If you want to experience more of my books, do join my Facebook readers group where you can chat to other readers and discuss my books, as well as anything else you are reading. I am very active in this group, and you can expect book jokes, puzzles, riddles, quizzes, giveaways, the opportunity to name characters, as well as secret information about what I'm working on, cover reveals and so much more!

Just click here: https://www.facebook.com/groups/
840324970233576

Read on for the first chapter of the next origin story, **_Sawyer Watson_**.

FREEBIE

If you'd like to read the next book in the series for **FREE**, please sign up to my newsletter at

https://www.marisanoelle.com/subscribe/

(You'll also get a bonus scene set in the world of *Secrets of the Deep* from Wade's point of view!)

Don't forget there are 10 more companion novellas in the series:
Silver Melody
Matt Lawson
Joe Rucker
Erica Swiftfield
Paige Starling
Hal Small
Kyle Lewis
Sawyer Watson
Addison Shields
President Bear

Turn the page to read the first chapter of the next origin story, *Sawyer Watson*.

SAWYER MASON
An Unadjusteds Story
MARISA NOELLE

A boy without a home.

A secret that could destroy him.

A choice that will change everything.

Twelve-year-old Sawyer Watson escapes an abusive foster home and disappears into the city's forgotten streets, where survival means never trusting anyone. But one stormy night, when a stranger drops a bag of glowing pills, one desperate choice changes his life forever.

The pill is a nanite—illegal, unstable, and deadly. Instead of killing him, it gives Sawyer the power to move objects with his mind. Terrified of discovery, he hides his ability and uses it only to steal food and stay alive. But when President Bear declares mandatory enhancements for all citizens, Sawyer's undocumented, high-class nanite makes him a target.

On the run, Sawyer joins a band of fugitives hiding deep within the Great Woods. For the first time, he finds warmth, friendship, and the promise of belonging. Yet as rebellion brews, he must decide if his gift makes him a weapon—or something worth saving.

Can a boy who's only ever survived learn what it means to truly live?

SAWYER WATSON

CHAPTER 1

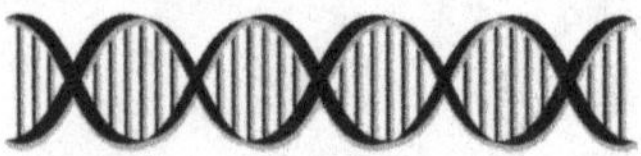

THE RAIN CUTS into Sawyer's skin like tiny glass shards. But it doesn't stop him running. His worn sneakers squelch in the unkempt lawn, each impact jarring the fresh bruises on his ribs. Twelve years old and running for his life— again. The third foster home this year, and maybe the worst.

Maybe. Hard to rank different flavors of nightmare.

After he rounds the corner of his block, he veers left down an alley, narrowly avoiding a stack of rotting boxes. He brushes the brick wall for balance, skin scraping against rough edges. The pain barely registers. Not after all the cigarette burns, or the purple welt stretching across his lower back from this morning's "discipline."

A car horn blares nearby. Sawyer ducks, pressing himself against a dumpster. *Stay quiet. Don't be seen. Survive another day.*

His t-shirt clings to his skin, soaked through and heavy. Water streams down his face, mixing with what might be tears if he still had any left to cry. But crying is for kids with options. Sawyer ran out of those a long time ago.

Five days ago, Mr. Reese came home drunk again. Nothing unusual there. But this time he caught Sawyer helping Milo with homework instead of finishing the dishes. The rage was swift and brutal.

"Ungrateful little shit," Mr. Reese had slurred, his meaty hand closing around Sawyer's arm. "Think you can slack off in my house?"

The memory sends a fresh surge of adrenaline through Sawyer. He pushes away from the dumpster and forces himself to move.

He rounds another corner, splashing through a puddle that soaks his already drenched sneakers. The water is cold enough to make his teeth chatter.

The rain falls like bullets, sheets of water that limit visibility to a few feet ahead. Good. Makes it harder for anyone to follow. Not that anyone would bother. The system has plenty more to fill his empty bed.

Something catches in his throat. Not quite a sob, more like the ghost of one. He thinks of the backpack stashed under a freeway overpass three blocks from the house. Two t-shirts, a worn hoodie, a plastic bag of granola bars stolen one by one from the pantry over the last few weeks.

"Sawyer!"

The barrels through the rain, small and frightened. Sawyer freezes mid-step, his body going rigid. No. *No no no.*

"Sawyer!"

He turns slowly, already knowing what he'll see. *Who* he'll see.

Milo stands in the mouth of the alley, a tiny figure framed by distant streetlights. His pajamas are soaked, clinging to his skinny eight-year-old frame. His feet are bare, pale against the dark pavement. His chestnut curls are plastered to his forehead, water dripping from his chin.

"Go back," Sawyer calls, his voice cracking. "Milo, go back to the house."

Milo takes a step forward, his small face crumpling. "Take me with you."

The words stab into Sawyer's chest. It takes every ounce of willpower to shake his head. "I can't."

"Please." Milo's voice breaks on the word. He takes another step forward, his bare feet splashing in a puddle. "Please, Saw."

The nickname nearly undoes him. Saw-boy, Milo calls him sometimes, when nightmares wake him and Sawyer is the only one who comes to check.

"You can't come with me," Sawyer says, forcing steel into his voice. "I don't have anywhere to go. I can't take care of you. It's too dangerous."

"I don't care," Milo insists, tears mixing with rainwater on his cheeks. "I want to go with you."

Sawyer closes his eyes for a second, fighting the urge to run back, to grab Milo's hand, to promise him everything will be okay. But that would be the biggest lie of all. Two kids on the street? They'd be found by social services within days. Or worse.

"Sawyer, don't leave me!" Milo's plea echoes through the rain-drenched alley, cutting straight through to whatever's left of Sawyer's heart.

Guilt twists inside him like a living thing, clawing at his insides. He should never have let Milo get attached. Should have kept his distance like with all the others. But there was something about the kid. His endless questions, his missing front tooth, the way he still believed good people existed despite everything.

"I'm sorry," Sawyer whispers, too quiet for Milo to hear through the rain.

He forces himself to turn away. Forces his feet to move, one step, then another. Each step feels like ripping open a fresh wound.

Behind him, Milo calls his name again, voice higher with panic. Sawyer clenches his jaw so tight it aches, bites down on the inside of his cheek until he tastes blood. Physical pain is easier. Physical pain makes sense.

He rounds the corner, breaking the line of sight. Milo's cries fade beneath the steady drumming of rain. Sawyer runs faster now, legs pumping, lungs burning. Running from Milo's voice. Running from the guilt.

He learned long ago that love is a luxury kids like him can't afford. Every time he's dared to care about someone, they've been taken away. Or they've hurt him. Or both. Safety is just another lie adults tell to make themselves feel better about the world they've created.

The only constant is survival. Keep moving. Stay invisible. Trust no one.

Sawyer swallows hard, forcing down the lump in his throat. He'll make it up to Milo somehow. Maybe once he's figured things out, found a way to survive on his own, he can come back for him.

But he knows it's a lie even as he thinks it. There's no going back. Only forward, into the rain, into the night, into whatever waits for him beyond the boundaries of another failed home.

His sneakers pound against the wet pavement, a rhythm like a heartbeat. The bruises throb. The rain falls. And Sawyer disappears into the storm.

After a couple of hours, Sawyer's lungs burn as he crests the final hill. The rain has finally stopped, but he is still soaked through. He slows to catch his breath, hands braced against his knees. The city stretches before him. A sprawling maze of steel and glass and concrete, its edges blurred by the hazy aftermath of the storm. Not a sanctuary. It's the only place he can think of to disappear.

He straightens, wincing as his bruised ribs scream. The sky is shifting from black to a dull, metallic gray, dawn still an hour away. Perfect timing. Easier to disappear in the pre-morning crush of early workers than the emptiness of night.

He pats his pocket, feeling the reassuring outline of the switchblade he stole from Mr. Reese's drawer. Not for using on people. Just for protection. At least that's what he tells himself.

Sawyer starts down the hill, each step jarring his exhausted body. The city grows larger, swallowing the horizon. Buildings stack atop each other like children's blocks arranged by a giant with no concept of order or beauty. Some stretch so high they disappear into low-hanging clouds, their tops invisible. Others squat and spread, taking up entire blocks.

As he gets closer, the digi-boards come into focus.

Massive screens plastered across buildings, shifting and pulsing with light. Even at this hour, they flash with constant motion—advertisements, most of them about nanites.

A woman's face fifty feet tall smiles down at him, her teeth impossibly white, her skin glowing with unnatural perfection. "Evolution is a choice," her voice booms across the empty street. "EvolveMe—be your best self."

The image shifts to a man in a business suit, his eyes an electric blue that no human is born with. "Class Six intelligence enhancement. Because in today's market, natural just isn't enough."

Sawyer snorts. As if anyone has a choice. Like nanites that rewrite DNA are meant for kids who crash in emergency shelters and eat whatever they can swipe. Those signs aren't for him. They're for the adjusteds—the shiny ones, the rebuilt ones, the people rich enough to buy a better version of themselves.

He passes beneath a flickering streetlamp, its light catching on the fresh scabs across his knuckles. Funny how the same society that creates miracle cures and superhuman abilities still can't be bothered to fix broken foster systems or abusive homes.

The digi-boards grow more numerous as he approaches the city center. A teenage boy with butterfly wings sprouting from his shoulders. "Class-Three aesthetic enhancement. Because ordinary is a choice." A woman lifting a car with one hand. "Bulk nanites! Strength beyond limits." A child with glowing fingertips that paint light in the air. "Give your child the gift of evolution."

Sawyer's seen adjusteds before, of course. His last school

had plenty. Rich kids with enhanced vision who never needed glasses, athletes with reflexes too quick to be natural, even a girl who could change her hair color just by thinking about it. They stayed away from the foster kids. As if poverty might be contagious.

The first commuters begin to appear. Early shift workers hurrying with heads down, the occasional business type already barking into wrist-comms. Sawyer hunches his shoulders, makes himself small.

He veers off the main street into a narrow alley between two looming buildings. The smell hits him immediately. Urine and rotting food and something worse beneath it all. But it's safer here, away from curious eyes and security cams that might flag a kid wandering alone.

Rain puddles reflect fragments of neon from the signs above, creating broken mirrors at his feet. Sawyer steps carefully around them, superstitiously avoiding his own reflection. He knows it's not pretty.

A blast of warm air catches him by surprise. There's a ventilation grate in the sidewalk pushing up steam from some underground system. Sawyer pauses over it, letting the heat seep into his damp clothes. For one moment, the constant chill retreats from his bones.

He follows the alley until it opens onto a small plaza squeezed between buildings. An overhang juts from one structure, providing shelter from the light drizzle that has started again.

Sawyer huddles beneath it, back pressed against the wall, knees drawn to his chest.

From here, the city puts its priorities on full display. Up

top, the polished towers, all glass and self-importance, packed with the enhanced. Down here, the rest of them claw through garbage for dinner. Two worlds, same city. One gets privilege. The other gets the leftovers.

He hugs himself tighter, trying to preserve what little body heat remains. Kids like him don't get rebuilt. They get forgotten, misplaced in the system, aged out into homelessness. They don't become butterflies or superheroes or geniuses. They become shadows.

A drop of water slides down his neck, making him shiver. Sawyer pulls his damp hood up. Above him, the ads continue their silent parade of impossible transformations. Below, his stomach growls.

He needs to find food. A place to dry his clothes. Somewhere to sleep that won't get him picked up by the cops. The city offers all these things, but none of them for free.

Nothing is ever free.

To carry on reading, click here:
https://geni.us/SawyerWatson